A STORM OF FORBIDDEN FEELING . . .

He towered over her, and Marion was acutely aware of his manly charms, broad shoulders, the strong, clean-shaven jaw, the hooked nose. His sharp, gray gaze penetrated to her very soul, and her heartbeat escalated. *Something*, an unspoken communication, passed between them, making Marion's knees melt . . .

Also by Maria Greene

LOVER'S KNOT

Daring Gamble

Maria Greene

DIAMOND BOOKS, NEW YORK

DARING GAMBLE

A Diamond Book / published by arrangement with
the author

PRINTING HISTORY
Diamond edition / May 1992

ISBN: 1-55773-708-8

Diamond Books are published by The Berkley Publishing Group,
200 Madison Avenue, New York, New York 10016.
The name "DIAMOND" and its logo are trademarks
belonging to Charter Communications, Inc.

PRINTED IN THE UNITED STATES OF AMERICA

10 9 8 7 6 5 4 3 2 1

Dedicated to my parents,
Runar and Helmy Staffans,
with love.

Thank you, Garda Parker.

Daring Gamble

CHAPTER 1

Dearest Papa,

I hate London. Why did you have to send me here? The city reeks with foul smells, and the air is gray with soot; the noise deafens me, and on the streets the crowds abuse my ears with the worst vocabulary imaginable. Aunt Adele is trying halfheartedly to treat me well, and I wish I could say the same about Uncle Bertram. They feel they have been saddled with an impossible task—to marry me off to some eligible gentleman. But their efforts have abated since Sir Cedric Longpole began showing such a blatant interest in me. However, I fear they silently pity him. He only wants me because of my inheritance.

As you probably recall, Uncle Bertram's town house is filled with treasures of all kinds, but it is so *gloomy*. The best room is the well-stocked library, even if it's frightfully disorganized. It might make you upset to hear that I'm still obsessed with reading and that no handsome beau has yet stolen my heart, but I have to be honest. The balls bore me to death, and the members of the *beau monde* are superficial and vain. Especially the ladies, but even the gentlemen dress to outshine each other, shirt-points so high they can't turn their heads and coats so tight it takes at least two assistants to force the garments on their backs. (Odious Melvin disclosed that little secret.)

Perchance you chuckle and say that at least I have noticed the opposite gender and that it's a step in the right direction, but the dismay I feel frightens me. Your suggestion that I should accept Sir Cedric's offer makes me shudder with revulsion. My humblest apologies for such ungratefulness, but the prospect is intolerable, and I beg of you not to insist that I marry that toad-faced gentleman. You know I can't be anything but repelled by his advances. The fact that you see him as a favorable candidate for my hand saddens me no end.

Oh, how I miss Somerset! More than I can say—the sweet air, the sun, and yes, even the humidity. London is damp in a cold, inhospitable way. The dank air crawls through every crack and crevice to make me miserable. Aunt Adele maintains that London soon will take on its bright spring face, and she tells me not to be so glum.

Dear Papa, to return to the subject of husbands, how can I find one to my liking with spectacles perched on the tip of my nose? And you know that I'm blind without them. None of the other debutantes wear spectacles, and they are all so pretty in a pink and white way—blond curls dressed in the latest styles, dimples, blue eyes, fluttering eyelashes. Papa, you know that I have none of those assets.

Even Cousin Melvin, of all people, sports dimples. He acts like a veritable debutante. Revolting! He aspires to becoming a dandy, although the title "debutante" suits him better, what with his mincing ways. If he ever reads this, he'll kill me. You might not know it, but he's a vicious sort of worm. I know you will berate me for slandering my relatives in this reckless manner, but, Papa, it's God's truth.

Last night I began counting my freckles but had to stop when I reached five hundred, and that was only one half of my face. And nobody has hair as bold as mine. People stare, and the other day an urchin cried for all the street to hear that my hair was on fire. You must understand my utter humiliation.

I suffer. Why won't you let me come home? How can you continue to deny my pleas? I don't mind dwindling into an old maid as long as I'm surrounded by the people I love, and my dear books.

Your Dutiful Daughter, Marion.

Miss Marion Rothwell's trembling fingers folded the stiff cream paper. Still seething with anger at the injustice of her forced stay in London, she wrote the address on the envelope: Sir Horace Rothwell, Rothwell Court, Burnham, Somerset. After throwing the letter on the table, she began restlessly pleating the fabric of her morning gown. Her stays chafed and pins dug into her skull when all she wanted was to let her hair hang freely over her shoulders and wear any old gown—any *comfortable* gown. And this silly pink satin ribbon under her breasts, ends fluttering and dipping into everything, it was too annoying to describe. Why, only yesterday she drenched one end in the tea cup and Aunt Adele almost had one of her fainting spells. Marion chuckled with glee; she knew she had brought her aunt almost to the brink of collapse, not a mean feat considering that she'd been in the Winthrop household on Albemarle Street only four weeks. Perhaps she would be sent home again. She glanced up from the desk in the study when her uncle stepped inside.

"There you are, m'dear," Uncle Bertram greeted her with forced joviality. He glanced with disapproval at her use of his desk and his writing implements, but she liked this room with its smell of books and old leather. She sensed his dislike, and it made her shrink.

He glanced at the envelope, the buttons of his tight waistcoat threatening to pop. Mr. Ponsonby, of Ponsonby and Sons, the Rothwell solicitor, entered behind him. She had known Archibald Ponsonby all her life. She rose instantly, but Uncle Bertram urged her to sit down. Waiting for them to speak, Marion glanced suspiciously from his heavy-jowled face to the solicitor's round one.

"I'm afraid I have some distressing news, my dear," said Mr. Ponsonby gently.

"Has something happened to Father?" Marion went icy all over, and cold sweat broke out on her back.

"Don't worry yourself, Miss Marion, but your father had an attack of sorts, an apoplexy. As you well know, his health has always been weak." He gave her a calming gesture, his eyes kind over the rim of his spectacles. "He's resting peacefully. In fact, when I visited him three days ago, he was sitting on the terrace in a Bath chair very much improved. He insisted that you not worry. Mrs. Halsey takes care—"

"What brought on the attack?" A wave of unease went through her. Something was wrong; she could feel it. Her thoughts swirled in confusion. "Well? What has Papa done now?" However much she loved her parent, she also worried about his haphazard management of the vast Rothwell holdings. The estate would go to her cousin Julian Rothwell upon her father's death, but her legacy was elsewhere—in her sire's dubious care. She was the proud owner of a lovely mansion called Laurel Manor and one thousand fertile acres that bordered to Rothwell Court. Her father had invested her sizable bequest from her mother in Laurel Manor. He had the kindest, most generous heart but also a reckless streak that always gave her cause for anxiety. There was no use denying it: Papa did not possess the most solid character; he had the reckless streak of a gambler. "Well?"

Mr. Ponsonby looked surprised. "What do you mean, Miss Marion? As far as I know, he had the attack at home. As I said, you shouldn't worry about him, but naturally, I had to inform you of his recent illness. He didn't want me to tell you, but I insisted. However, he stipulated that under no circumstances are you to travel back to Burnham because of him. He's in the good hands of a hired nurse."

She wanted to know more, but Uncle Bertram insisted that her aunt required a word with her in the morning room, and Marion had to give in. Mr. Ponsonby stood as she moved and patted her hand. "Don't worry, Miss Marion, everything will be fine."

Her father was ill, but why? Had some serious upset brought on the attack? Why couldn't she lose the premonition of disaster, she wondered as she lingered in the hallway. What was the solicitor holding back?

She viewed the image of herself in a girandole mirror by the door. A pale transparent ghost with burning green eyes stared back at her. Her mop of frizzy curls mocked her like the red flames of hell.

Marion sighed and watched the rain sloshing against the windows. An umbrella bobbed up and down outside, and she leaned forward to take a look at the victim of the downpour: Melvin Winthrop, her odious cousin, whom she had made an instant enemy upon arriving in London. She had presented him a handsome pair of riding gloves only to discover that he abhorred horses and didn't like female cousins usurping his parents' affection.

So as not to ruin the sheen of his gleaming Hessians, he tiptoed between the puddles. Marion snorted with disapproval. A strong urge to play a prank came over her. Perhaps she could catch a mouse or a toad and hide it in his bed. But such childish urges would have to be suppressed from now on. She was a lady now, and everyone expected her to behave like one. Her aunt had despaired of the "wild hoyden" that had arrived in London. She had pronounced with a moan, "I shall never get the chit off my hands!"

Marion's thoughts reluctantly turned to Sir Cedric Longpole. No wonder the young man had attached himself to *her*, the ugliest girl in London, since all the debutantes shunned him. With that pockmarked face of his and shifty eyes, he would never impress a beauty. Marion shivered. "Ugh!" she directed at the painting of some obscure forefather on the wall. "Where will I find the courage to turn down Sir Cedric, especially now that Papa is ill? How can I refuse Papa's wishes when he's in a weakened condition?"

With her freckles, she would never have to worry about being inundated with other proposals of marriage. "But you know I cannot marry Sir Cedric. He not only looks like a toad, but has the disposition of one. *Nobody* could wish me such a fate," she complained to the sour-faced forefather.

If she gave in to everyone's wishes, she would be Sir Cedric's wife before the end of the Season, a fate worse than death. Only just eighteen years old, Marion had no desire to die, although sometimes her despair appeared to be killing her bit by bit.

In a desperate situation, some desperate measure would have to be taken, but a different one than her relatives were planning. She would not marry Sir Cedric!

Tears running silently down her cheeks, Marion opened the letter in her hand once more. Her fingers clutched the paper and her tears splashed the script, diluting the ink as she added a few lines to the bottom of the page.

Dearest Papa,

It saddens me to inform you that I'm going to disobey your wish. I cannot possibly reconcile myself to the idea of marrying Sir Cedric. I'm sorry. Please don't judge me too harshly.

Her movements were sluggish as she sealed the envelope. Her thoughts were running in ever-tighter circles, and she finally realized that she would have to come up with an excuse to visit her father. She *had to* see him. Uncle Bertram would try to dissuade her, but if he didn't know . . .

She viewed the letter thoughtfully, then tore it up with a decisive twist of her hands. A flutter of new strength manifested in her heart. Perhaps her father, weak after the attack, wouldn't be so set on her spending the entire spring in London. Once he saw her in person, he wouldn't have the strength to send her back. She would persuade him that he needed her.

That night when everyone slept, and after donning a few borrowed garments from Melvin's wardrobe, Marion sneaked down the stairs. She carefully counted the steps, avoiding the ones that creaked. In one hand she carried a portmanteau and in the other the cage with her parrot Prinny, nicknamed after the Prince of Wales. She prayed fervently that the inhabitant of the cloth-covered cage would keep silent, at least until she rounded the corner of Albemarle Street.

As she slipped out the front door a link boy hurried past, followed by two sprigs of fashion. Arm in arm they wove across the street singing at the top of their lungs. A movement in the gilt cage told her that Prinny had been awakened by the noise and was ruffling his feathers.

"Squawk. Squuuaawk."

"Be quiet, you silly featherhead. We'll be detected posthaste if you keep this up," Marion whispered and hastened along the silent street.

"Devilish nuisance!" came the gloomy voice from the cage.

Marion giggled nervously. The poor bird could not help possessing a vulgar vocabulary, not after spending twenty years in Great-Uncle Simon Rothwell's company. She could not dream of leaving her pet behind as she fled from an impossible fate.

After the afternoon rainshower the cobblestones glistened wet and treacherous beneath her feet, and as Marion turned the corner of Grafton Street, she stumbled and crashed headlong to the ground. The cage bounced over the stones just as a curricle and team came bowling down the street.

Marion screamed, her fear focusing on the cage, its black cover flapping wildly.

"Damnation!" squeaked the bird as the cage hit the foundation of the house on the opposite side of the street. "Blasted hedgebird!"

Whinnying as the bits jarred their sensitive mouths, the horses stopped inches from Marion, who was sprawled on the grimy stones. Harnesses jingled, hooves fretted perilously close to her head, and snorts tortured her ears. Petrified, Marion dimly noticed a pair of sturdy short legs stepping over her body.

"A close 'un, guv'," came the nasal but youthful tones of a native Londoner. "Gorblimey, looka 'ere, a bleedin' cull on 'is belly!"

Her nostrils assaulted by the potent odor of sweating horsehide, Marion watched another pair of legs jumping out of the curricle. Tight topboots encased muscular calves, hinting at the long legs hidden behind a voluminous driving coat with many capes.

Marion's legs were jellylike as a pair of strong hands pulled her to her feet. The man peered closely at her in the darkness. "A mere stripling! What are you doing out in the middle of the night? Don't you know that footpads lurk in dark doorways and alleys?" scolded his deep melodious voice.

Marion made her voice deliberately gruff, imitating a boy. "What are *you* doing abroad, then, if it is so hazardous?" she bit back. "Perchance you are one of those dreaded individuals." Without waiting for an answer, she continued, "Prinny! Is Prinny hurt?"

Large hands brushed off her pantalooned legs and coattails. Frantically, she pushed them away before he reached her feminine curves.

"Prinny? Th' cove's a looby," judged the urchin at her elbow.

"Please, my bird–" She staggered across the street to retrieve the cage. Prinny was hanging upside down on his perch, his head cocked to one side as he peered at Marion in the weak light from the sliver of moon playing hide and seek with the heavy clouds. "Devil take it all! Ha-ha-ha-haha."

"Rum goings on, guv', th' lad 'as lost 'is marbles. Let's leave while we can." The urchin impatiently jangled one of the bridles, and the horses whickered.

The man in the caped coat did not respond but stepped decisively across the street. "May I be of further assistance?" His voice held disapproval. "As I said, you should not be abroad in the middle of the night. Appears to me like you're running away."

"I am, and I would appreciate it if you'd stop berating me for my foolishness. I got enough of that where I came from.'' Marion studied him and noticed that he stood very tall. His easy bearing and voice spoke of a relatively young man. For unknown reasons, his closeness created no fear within her, although the street was quite deserted.

''Sir, you may give me a lift to the White Stag Inn, where I can catch the coach to Bath. That's the least you can do after nearly killing me,'' she added.

He laughed, a dry derisive sound. ''Oh, and you're perfectly without blame, I take it?''

''Of course. I was only minding my own business while you tore down the street at neck or nothing. Perhaps you ran over a few night revelers on your way here—even killed one—and at this very moment are escaping your just punishment.'' Standing on her toes, she thrust her eyes close to his face and discerned a gleam of white teeth. ''Well?''

''You possess a lively imagination, stripling.'' He slapped his gloves against his thigh. His voice quivered slightly with suppressed mirth. ''Unfortunately, you're quite mistaken. In fact, I'm called out of town on very dull business, and I assure you that no drunkards lost their lives at my hands tonight.''

''Heave to, lads!'' urged Prinny.

''Sssh, you silly bird.'' Marion hastened to drape the cage with the black cloth. ''Pay no heed to Prinny, sir. He has the most distressing manners. My great-uncle was an admiral and taught him a shocking vocabulary. In fact, the old feathermop would have lost his life because of his speech had I not taken pity on him.''

''I see. A particularly good deed on your part, then.'' The man walked back to the restive horses. ''Well, stripling, I suppose I should call the Watch and have you taken to the bosom of your family, but by some peculiar reason I feel a reluctance to do so if they are as mean as you imply.''

Marion rushed after him. ''They truly are! And worse.

My uncle is the most tedious man alive, and my cousin is the silliest clod in Mayfair.''

''I suppose I'm doing a good deed, then.''

She inhaled deeply. ''Thank you, sir, I will always remember your kindness. And now, if you could only take me to the inn. I want to go home to my—er—fath—parents in . . . in Bath,'' she lied glibly. ''You said yourself it's dangerous to be abroad at night,'' she hastened to remind him as she sensed his hesitation.

He climbed lithely into the vehicle and pulled on his gloves. ''As a matter of fact I'm heading out the Bath road myself.'' Mockery tinted his voice as he added, ''And if you think a lift is payment enough for nearly killing you, I'm prepared to take you to the White Stag Inn, even though it's sheer madness.''

''That is no more than your due, after all,'' Marion concluded roundly. She sneaked a glance at his dark profile to see if her words had annoyed him, but his expression gave nothing away. His hands closed calmly and competently around the ribbons as he took control of the team.

The fine horses and the elegant curricle proved that he was a member of polite society. Had she perhaps met him at one of the routs or balls, even danced with him? An unlikely possibility, since she was the perennial wallflower of those gatherings.

The urchin, obviously the man's tiger, proceeded to sweep a cloak around Prinny's cage. With a virulent curse the boy hoisted it up on his perch at the back of the vehicle. ''We can't have the bird catch a cold, can we?'' the gentleman commented as Marion anxiously observed the urchin's movements.

''Sir, I don't want to appear nosy, but may I inquire your name?''

''I suppose it's in order since we're going to be traveling

companions for a while. Pierce Litton at your service.'' He let the horses have their heads and they flew over the cobblestones.

''Litton? The Earl of Edgewater?'' Filled with incredulity Marion stared at her companion. ''The Catch of the Season?''

He laughed. ''Is that what they call me? Well, let me inform you, I will not get *caught* this Season or any other. I have eluded that horrifying fate so far.''

Marion went into paroxysms of gruff laughter. ''You're very entertaining, milord. Excuse my sudden hilarity, but I pictured all the pink and white beauties sitting along various ballroom walls armed with fishing rods.''

''Pink and white? Fishing rods?''

''Yes, milord, haven't you noticed that all the debutantes wear those colors, and sport dimples on the right side of their faces? And they sit along the walls with intent expressions as if they were fishing.''

Lord Edgewater laughed. ''No, I had not realized the fact, but now that you're pointing it out to me—By the way, how do you know so much about debutantes, stripling? You must be barely out of shortcoats.''

''Ahem . . . my—my sister Marion is one.''

''Pink and white?''

''Oh—no!'' Marion shuddered. ''She's *ugly*, with hair the color of a bonfire, and she wears spectacles.''

''Tedious, indeed. I vaguely remember a bonfire in some ballroom, but then all the debutantes look alike to me, bonfire or not. They can be very tiresome, I might add. Now, who do I have the pleasure—?'' Edgewater asked.

Concealing her real name, Marion introduced herself. ''I'm . . . er, Martin Rockwall.''

''Your most obedient, et cetera, et cetera.'' He shot her a glance. ''Harrow? Eton?''

Marion almost panicked. What would she say if he started prying into the names of her schoolmates? "Harrow, milord." She clutched his arm. "Say, do you like books?"

"I'd say I'm rather more the sporting type, but I daresay I've read a few. Why?" He turned a corner with hairpin precision, and the horses raced north on Bond Street.

"*I* love books." Marion waited breathlessly for him to agree.

He chuckled. "Quite the scholar, hey? Keeps you out of mischief at school. You evidently don't shirk classes for a day of fishing. I used to always choose the fishing, although we had difficulty finding worms close to school. They were all used up."

Marion shivered. "Ugh! How can you talk about such dreadful creatures?" Too late did she see her mistake. She felt his eyes probing her face for a brief moment.

"I thought only females harbored an aversion to worms."

Marion sucked in her breath sharply. "Er? . . . Yes, of course. I was only roasting you, milord."

The tiger saved her by tapping the earl on the shoulder. "'Ere, ye should turn 'ere, guv'. Th' White Stag comin' up, at Uxfor' Street."

Already far from home, Marion feared leaving the safety of the earl's company. Blackness still shrouded the world, and the few candles gleaming in windows created a flickering eeriness. The silence bore a threatening quality, and a rivulet of unease snaked through her.

As if he sensed her discomfort, the earl turned to Marion. "This is not promising. The inn is bound to be full at this hour. Let us continue to Maidenhead and there break our journey. You can catch the stagecoach there tomorrow morning."

"Thank you, milord. I'm most grateful." Relaxing once more, Marion fought to keep her eyelids open. Such an eventful night, and such distinguished company! The other debutantes would be green with envy if they knew that Marion Rothwell at this very moment was nestling close to the most eligible man in London. No one she knew had ever been fortunate enough to gain a drive in the earl's curricle.

The clothes she had borrowed from Melvin had successfully filled their purpose, shielding her from unwelcome advances. By the time Lord Edgewater awakened tomorrow, she would be long gone, and he none the wiser as to her true gender.

A thought struck her. "Why is it that you use a quizzing glass to stare at people at the balls?" she asked sleepily. "Your eye looks hideously distorted through it. Is your sight impaired?"

The earl barked a sudden laugh. "I believe my sight has not yet dimmed with age." He silenced as if in thought. "The quizzing glass has many uses. A magnified eye can be disconcerting to toad-eaters and disagreeable persons in general, and one can swing it on the ribbon to alleviate boredom, something I often feel, I might add."

"Oh. Well, I'm blind without my spectacles . . . just like my sister."

A gust of wind whipped the beaver hat from Marion's head, and she threw herself after it, almost falling out of the curricle in the process. The earl's hand gripped her arm tightly. "Are you desiring an untimely end?"

"My hat!" She patted her flattened hair nervously, praying he would not notice the feminine style.

The dreary damp cold of the night worsened as big raindrops began splashing the flanks of the horses, teasing the leaves of the trees lining the road and wetting Marion's cheeks.

"Come here, lad. This won't do. I don't want to be accused at some future date of letting you contract pneumonia.'' With one sweep of his arm, Edgewater covered her with a cloak and pulled her closer to himself to infuse some warmth into her numb limbs. Protected from the rain, Marion snuggled gratefully against his body.

To the steady clip-clop of the horses' hooves, she drifted off to sleep. With her ear pressed to the earl's chest, she was faintly aware of his voice resonating strangely in her ear.

''How the devil did you know that I carry a quizzing glass?''

CHAPTER

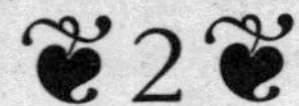

THE BOAT SWAYED GENTLY AS MARION OPENED ONE BLEARY EYE, dimly realizing the vessel was a pair of strong arms. Cautiously opening the other eye, she saw the underside of a strong jaw, darkly shadowed by a night's growth of beard, and a starched cravat. Someone said, "The lad's a heavy sleeper, but when he finds out that I *carried* him inside as if he were a girl, his hackles will be up. Please don't tell him."

Marion gasped and stiffened. A pair of calm gray eyes looked down at her face.

"Jolly good, Rockwall! You're awake."

"Where are we?" she addressed the handsome eyes.

"At The George in Maidenhead." He set her down in what looked like a private parlor, and she rubbed her eyes with her knuckles.

The room was Tudor style, wattle and daub walls, the ceiling low and beamed, and the wide floorboards slanting slightly. The furniture looked clumsy and uncomfortable.

"I must have dropped off to sleep." Forgetting her manners, she yawned hugely. Her attention was captured and held by one gray eye, enormous through the quizzing glass. His disconcerting gaze proceeded to travel the length of her body.

"By thunder! I believe you pulled the wool over my

eyes,'' Lord Edgewater intoned flatly. ''I surmise your name is not Martin, but Martina. What don't females do to snare an unsuspecting gentleman! This charade surely takes the prize.'' He dropped the quizzing glass and it swung across his pearl-gray silk waistcoat.

Marion sensed his great—and for the moment barely suppressed—anger. She decided to take a frank approach to this new development. ''I suppose the game is up, eh? My name is Marion Rothwell, and I'm the bespectacled sister of the fictitious brother I invented last night, but at least I got away—''

''Say no more!'' he spat through clenched teeth. The earl raised the palm of his hand to stem any further verbal onslaught. ''What infernal cheek!'' He led her to a chair and made her sit down. Seating himself, he ordered a tankard of ale and breakfast from the gawking host.

As they were left alone, the earl's hard gaze pinned Marion until she cringed with discomfort, and his voice echoed profound irritation as he continued.

''I presume you laid in wait for me and threw yourself in front of the horses, what? Blast it!'' The curse flowed unchecked from his lips, and Marion didn't blame him for his anger. For a gentleman to spend the night with an unchaperoned, unwed lady was unthinkable. The only honorable thing he could do was to offer her marriage. Marion tried to interrupt his tirade, but he went on.

''Such tiresome business. I've just left such a situation in London where a lady tried to gain my name by entrapment. However, I saw through her ruse at the last moment.'' He stared hard at Marion, and her cheeks grew hot with embarrassment. ''If you're planning to return to London crying that I abducted you and that I have to wed you to silence the scandal, you're making a big mistake.''

Astonished, Marion looked into his narrowed eyes, where

a dangerous gleam burned. She yawned undauntedly, then said, "I have no idea what you're talking about, milord. Truly." She looked out the window as a misty dawn reluctantly manifested. "I have no interest in you. I'm only anxious to board the coach to Bath."

The drowsy landlord returned, his thick arms bearing a tray laden with ale and a plate of cold meat, kedgeree, boiled eggs, and a loaf of white bread. Silence hung heavy in the room and the earl's suspicious glare kept boring into her, but Marion was too sleepy to be intimidated by his wrath.

Directing her weary gaze at the landlord, she said, "When is the westbound stagecoach due?"

"At eight o'clock, sir." His gaze darted from one "gentleman" to the other. "But I'm quite sure I saw you arrive in a private conveyance."

"Our roads will part here. Please, reserve an inside seat for me," Marion pleaded, pulling out a purse from the pocket of Melvin's coat. Aware of her legs so blatantly displayed in tight buff pantaloons, she blushed fiercely. *Oh, dear.* Squaring her shoulders, she struggled for an authoritative air as she counted out the required fare. "That will be all, thank you." She meticulously avoided Lord Edgewater's eyes. One of the maids carried Prinny's cage into the room.

Once more alone with the earl, Marion turned her back on him and stared out the window.

"You were right, it does look like a bonfire."

Marion whirled around, flushed and tight-lipped. "Then you see how preposterous your suspicion is! Why would I be waiting in a dark street to nab a husband, least of all *you*? I didn't know you were driving that way. Besides, no gentleman likes a bluestocking."

His lips quivered, and she perceived that the storm had

left his eyes. "With pantaloons you don't need to wear stockings, blue or otherwise."

Marion shrugged. "I would not have reached this far in petticoats, any fool can see that." She eyed him with candid curiosity. The Earl of Edgewater was as attractive as she remembered from the balls she had attended. She didn't know his age. He must be more than five-and-twenty, but no more than thirty. His face held no classic beauty, yet he was—she searched for the right word—striking. His jet-hued hair, brushed back and curling over the collar of his coat, framed a lean, harsh-featured face with a thin, straight nose and wide, sensuous lips. The black stubble on the determined jaw lent him a rakish air but failed to lighten the grooves of habitual boredom etched from nose to lips. His hard level gaze had the power to unsettle a less innocent individual than she. Yet she knew that sudden laughter could dispel the iciness in those eyes, as they twinkled now.

"A fool, am I? Yes, I've been labeled that many times. Now, since you have convinced me that you're not trying to get me leg-shackled, we might as well share the repast and get on with our business." He eased his broad shoulders from the chair and heaped food on a plate, placing it before her. "You are a most unusual lady. In fact, I don't think I've ever met anyone like you."

Marion eyed the food with relish, clapping her hands. "Breakfast is most welcome." She broke off a piece of bread. "Is it rude to inquire what business brings you out on the roads in the middle of the night?" she asked between bites.

"I was just about to ask the same question. Our meeting was unconventional, to say the least. I know I have no right to pry, but when a young *female* jaunts about the countryside, it makes me wonder." Lord Edgewater drank deeply from the tankard. "I told you before, I have an urgent but dull business matter that needs my immediate attention. I couldn't sleep, so I decided to get an early start. Now, what about you?''

''I assure you I'm not in the habit of traveling on the King's highway dressed in . . . ahem, breeches and tailcoat.'' She sighed deeply to regain her crumbling composure. ''But be that as it may. Tell me, what would *you* do if you looked like this''—she pointed at her thin freckled face—''and was never asked to dance?''

A glum answer came from the cage, ''Hang it all!'' Prinny ruffled his feathers, releasing a cloud of dust.

An unholy light shone in Lord Edgewater's eyes. ''I'm inclined to agree with the bird.''

Marion's lips twitched, and she sent the earl a shrewd glance. ''At least you give me an honest reply.'' To hide her sudden embarrassment she clawed through the contents of her portmanteau and pulled out an apple. Deftly she cut a wedge and handed it to the bird. ''Thank you,'' came the metallic response as Prinny's sharp talons closed around the fruit.

''If it makes you feel any better, I promise to dance with you at the next ball.''

Surprised, Marion glanced at him. ''Would you?'' She straightened abruptly. ''Very decent of you, milord. But I don't want your pity. Anyhow, I'm returning home to my estate to dwindle into spinsterhood.'' No self-pity colored her voice.

''Aha! So you lied to me about your parents in Bath. I take it you've slipped away from your guardian to take life into your own hands?'' The gleam in his eyes mocked her. ''Don't you think he'll be pursuing you to haul you back to London? He'll be worried when finding your bed empty.'' Lord Edgewater rolled his eyes heavenward. ''S'faith! The foolishness of youth.''

Marion chewed on her bottom lip. "I never thought of that. But then my uncle isn't forced to marry someone he abhors."

"Oh, I thought you had no luck with the gentlemen." The earl speared a piece of ham with his fork.

Anger blazed through her. "If you were *forced* to marry someone, I'm sure you'd run away as well."

He chuckled and rubbed his chin. Casually he said, "Most likely. Well, to get away from such a hideous fate, you could always wed me. To save you, I might offer myself to the martyrdom of marriage. That way I would be forever safe from the snares of match-making mamas. After all, I have compromised you by spending the night in your company." He made a gesture of protest when he noticed her ire.

Marion thought she would choke with mortification. "We didn't commit—" she began.

"Don't take me wrong!" he continued. Humor danced wickedly in his eyes, and his voice slowed to a drawl. "I know we didn't commit anything . . . forbidden. What sins could we have committed in the dismal rain? A most unromantic interlude, I admit. But we're in a deuced pickle; if this would come out—And I can't leave you to fend for yourself."

"I beg you not to worry your head about that, milord. I can take care of myself. No one will be the wiser, and since our roads will part in"—she looked at the clock on the mantelpiece—"half an hour, your anxieties will be over. And let me inform you, I haven't the slightest wish to marry you, or anyone else." She hunched her shoulders. "A husband would only forbid me to read my books—be a millstone around my neck."

He regarded her intently and swung his quizzing glass on

its ribbon. ''I had no idea your passion lies with crumbling printed tomes.''

''They are not crumbling! How could a person know *anything* without reading? And next you'll call me a bluestocking, I just know it.''

He shrugged. ''I don't care if you are. Mayhap the world would be a better place if females read a few books. It might take their minds off nagging us poor gentlemen to death.''

''Truly spoken by a gentleman,'' Marion mocked and gave her spectacles a determined push. ''How typical.'' She glowered at the grin parting his lips.

She ate in furious silence, counting the minutes to the arrival of the stage. She had long finished her breakfast and had almost paced a hole in the floor before the rumble of coach wheels and a blast from the yard of tin disrupted the silence of the peaceful morning outside. ''I daresay that this is the Bath coach.''

''Miss Rothwell, if you so desire, you may join me in my curricle to Bath, since that's my destination. I do enjoy your company, and I could protect you. Surely you'll be able to play the part of a boy all the way.''

''You surprise me, milord. I thought you were eager to be rid of me.'' Marion bent to retrieve her portmanteau. ''I thank you for your offer. But as you said, if my uncle or anybody else finds out that I'm traveling about the country with the Earl of Edgewater, my reputation will be in shreds and you'll be forced to wed me. No, let's pretend we never met.'' On those words, she hoisted the cage and turned toward the open door.

''Wait!'' Lord Edgewater strode to her side. ''Since I can't kiss your hand''—he glanced into the coffee room filling with people from the coach—''let me at least shake it.'' Taking the portmanteau, he clasped her hand warmly. ''At the next ball I'll be looking for a head of fire.''

"There will be no next time. I hate balls, and I'm not going back to London." Marion left the parlor, her shoulders tense.

Twenty minutes after the coach had left The George, Marion caught a glimpse of the earl as he bowled past the coach at reckless speed. If only she could have joined him! She digested the events of the previous night. How strange fate could be: Marion Rothwell driving through the darkness with the most brilliant catch of the Season, the Earl of Edgewater. He was considered wealthy beyond measure, and as slippery as an eel when it came to match-making mamas. Not only that, he had the reputation of a gamester, although that did not stop position-hungry parents pushing their daughters at him. Marion's lips curved upward as she imagined the moment she could tell Aunt Adele of this night's adventure. Her aunt would surely feign one of her Violent Spasms. Well, she could have as many spasms as she liked, Marion mused grimly.

The journey home to Burnham seemed endless. When Marion arrived at Rothwell Court only to find out from Mrs. Halsey, the housekeeper, that she would have to return to Bath to see her father, she groaned with fatigue.

"Dear Mrs. Halsey, no one told me that Father was taking the waters in Bath," she directed at the plump lady in the cavernous hall at Rothwell Court.

The housekeeper bristled with indignation. "I am not surprised! We didn't expect you home—especially not dressed like that! If I may say so, Miss Marion, you look a disgrace." Mrs. Halsey's long glance of disapproval settled on Marion's crumpled coat. "Mr. Ponsonby sent around a note saying he would be speaking with your father tomorrow on most urgent business. He requested my presence, and Thimble's. Whatever for, I have no idea, but you'd better join me, Miss Marion. He hinted at some legal business that concerned my usual position as housekeeper, not here, but at Laurel Manor. I don't know what he's talking about. I plan to return to Laurel once your father is better. That Ponsonby must have windmills in his head!''

''I will accompany you, Mrs. Halsey, but let me rest for a few hours. I swear I could not face another minute on the roads.''

''Of course. Not that I see why you had to take the stagecoach.''

''Lack of funds. Uncle Bertram gives me very little pin money, and Father forgot to send me my allowance.'' Marion dragged herself to bed, happy to be back home.

Marion stood by the open window of her old room and breathed the fresh morning air, the salty breeze the sea carried inland. This moment was worth all the discomfort the journey had caused her. After donning a shapeless muslin gown, she draped a paisley shawl over her shoulders and pulled a brush through her riotous red curls. Then she hastened along the gallery, where ancestors stared at her from the many portraits on the walls. She would tour the house, then visit her old pony in the stables.

Mrs. Halsey saw to it that the Louis XV furniture gleamed with weekly polishing and the oriental carpet was brushed. The tall windows glittered in the sunlight, and the ornate plaster moldings in the ceilings were freshly painted.

She said good morning to Thimble, the butler, as he carried a silver tray into the study. She frowned as she noticed the brandy carafe. Who would drink brandy so early in the morning?

At the bottom of the wide curving stairs she almost careened into the housekeeper.

''We don't have to make that trip to Bath, Miss Marion,''

Mrs. Halsey said with unusual distress. "Mr. Ponsonby arrived—"

"Oh, good. Is breakfast served in the breakfast parlor?" Without paying attention to Mrs. Halsey's frown, Marion steered her steps toward that cheerful room at the back of the house.

"Miss Marion, I believe Mr. Ponsonby and your father are awaiting your presence in the library."

"Papa is back, then?" Marion faced the old woman, premonition prickling her skin. "What is Mr. Ponsonby doing here?"

"I wouldn't know, Miss Marion, but Mr. Ponsonby looked very worried, and the man with him and your father in the study is real Quality if I'm not mistaken." The housekeeper wrung her hands in agitation.

"The man? What man?" Mrs. Halsey had Marion's full attention now.

"Oh, some toff in very handsome clothes and driving a team of excellent horseflesh, according to Pixby's own words. Old Pixie ought to know what he's talking about. Your father was very taken aback upon hearing you had returned home, miss. Unchaperoned."

Marion's lips curved into a faint smile. "I daresay. Not many people know that I have. Oh, dash it all! What did Papa say?"

"Nothing. He looked very sad."

"Hmmm." Marion chewed on her bottom lip. Dreading the interview, she steered her steps across the black and white checkered marble floor to the heavy oak door of the library. As she swung it wide, her heated words stuck in her throat. In her father's favorite leather chair sat none other than the Earl of Edgewater, twirling his quizzing glass. His eyes widened with surprise.

"You!" Marion exclaimed when she could find her voice.

His face lit up, but before he could answer, Mr. Ponsonby blurted out, "You two know each other?"

Pierce Litton, the Earl of Edgewater, turned to the rotund solicitor. "Eh . . . yes, I've danced once or twice with Miss . . . in London." His appreciative gaze crept the length of her body. "But I must say, she looks more fetching today than—than ever."

"That is a monstrous exaggeration, milord." She righted her spectacles and stared in confusion from one man to the other. Then she walked to her father, who was sitting in a Bath chair bundled in blankets, his shoulders hunched over. He looked unnaturally pale, his cheeks sunken, and his hands fleshless and trembling. She kissed his cheek and took one of his hands in her warm clasp. "Papa, darling," she whispered. He squeezed her fingers, evidently reluctant to look at her. She raised her voice authoritatively. "What brings you gentlemen here at this early hour of the morning?" Her mind reeling, she tried to figure out why—of all people—the Earl of Edgewater, was sitting in her father's favorite chair in the library. A sinking feeling of disaster settled upon her. She glanced at the well-filled bookcases lining the walls, as if looking for an answer.

"It distresses me no end to be the harbinger of further sad news, Miss Rothwell." Mr. Ponsonby's kindly blue eyes fastened on her as he lifted his gaze from a stack of papers on the desk. "Although we all know that Sir Horace is well liked in all circles and has a respectable reputation with the banks, a fact has come to light that will upset you greatly." He motioned to Marion to sit down. She sank down on the sofa, her gaze riveted to the old solicitor, her limbs numb with trepidation.

"Your father, before his illness, participated in a gamble

of rather large proportions.'' The words vibrated ominously in the air. When Marion did not seem to react, he continued after sending a furtive glance at Sir Horace's shrunken body. ''We also know that Sir Horace is wealthy, that Rothwell Court is a prosperous estate. As you well know, it's entailed and will go to your cousin in due course. However, your private inheritance, Laurel Manor, holds no encumbrance—'' He paused, and somehow Marion knew the words that would follow.

She whispered, ''He lost it. He gambled and lost my inheritance . . . Is that what you're trying to tell me?''

''Miss Marion, you know that most of your father's funds are tied up in Rothwell Court but that Laurel Manor was yours outright—under his guardianship until your eventual marriage.'' He paused, sending an apprehensive glance at Sir Horace, who seemed to have shrunk even more. ''All was well until this gentleman came with his claim.''

Marion started to speak, but Mr. Ponsonby held up his hand, urging her to wait. ''I swear upon my honor that I had no idea that Lord Edgewater held a claim to your estate.''

''Claim? I don't understand—''

''Dear Miss Marion, let me explain.'' The solicitor stepped around the desk, a piece of paper clamped between his fingers. She held it and read. Her father's curly writing style swam in front of her eyes.

''This is a promissory note, Miss Marion, and there is no doubt that this is your father's signature.'' His fat finger stabbed the note. ''All in all, your father lost Laurel Manor and all its land to Lord Edgewater—at a game of piquet.''

''Impossible!'' Marion's voice was a stiff whisper. ''Do you mean—'' Her hand fell limp into her lap. ''You mean . . . I have nothing?'' She pinned accusing eyes on Lord Edgewater.

''I'm afraid you haven't, Miss Marion,'' Ponsonby continued. "When your father signed this note, he made you penniless." The solicitor raked a shaking hand through his thin hair. "I had no idea until yesterday, when Lord Edgewater stepped into my office in Bath. I sent over a note to your father and Mrs. Halsey. The servants who used to work at Laurel Manor might have to leave."

"So this was your *dull* business matter." Marion glared at Edgewater, whom she had believed to be a true gentleman. She turned to Mr. Ponsonby, who gazed at her with deep sadness, and her words of protest died on her lips. The solicitor would never play a wicked prank on her, nor would her father, who looked more like a shadow every minute. Her eyes questioned Lord Edgewater, distress churning in her stomach.

His clear, gray gaze met hers. "I declare I had no idea," the earl murmured, his long fingers toying with the eyeglass. "I'm afraid your father likes deep play."

When Marion turned to question her sire, he only nodded, his eyes infinitely tired.

Marion stood, seething with fury. "Wretch!" she said to Lord Edgewater. "You obviously enjoy deep play as well, or you would not be the new owner of Laurel Manor!" Misery engulfed her, but she raised her chin proudly. She would not give him the pleasure of witnessing her tears.

"It distresses me to see your suffering, Miss Rothwell, and I could tear the promissory note in two, but—"

"No! I will not have it bandied about that Sir Horace Rothwell failed to pay his gambling debts." She thrust the promissory note into his hand. "Keep it. I will have my belongings removed from Laurel Manor promptly." Although she wanted to rush out of the room, she walked slowly to the door, her head held high.

"Miss Marion! What will you do now?" Mr. Ponsonby asked before she could exit.

"I have but one choice: I will return to London. Sir Bertram might try to force me into marriage with Sir Cedric Longpole to get rid of me, but I'll fight." Her eyes glittered with bitterness, and she opened the door. "Anyway, what gentleman wants to be saddled with a wife with no prospects? Perhaps Sir Cedric's ardor will dwindle with my new penniless state." On those words she closed the door softly behind her before they could speak.

The stairs swayed and disappeared in front of her eyes. Mrs. Halsey's comforting arm encircled her waist and, crooning, the old woman led Marion up the stairs. Upon reaching the sanctuary of her room, Marion fought her tears and addressed the servant. "I'm ruined. Lord Edgewater, the gentleman in the fine clothes, is the new owner of Laurel Manor. Papa lost everything at a hand of piquet. Mrs. Halsey, I had no idea that he was such a hardened gambler." She rubbed her eyes in despair.

"Oh, I suspected it. Ever since your mother died in that wasting illness, your father has been very unhappy, Miss Marion. And, if you excuse me, miss, he looked rather deeply into the brandy bottle." Mrs. Halsey crumpled a handkerchief between her hands. "We tried to keep those dark parts of his life from you, child. You must know that your father loves you dearly, even if he isn't as strong as he used to be. He's grown awfully forgetful of late. He doesn't seem to have any reason to live."

Marion nodded, suppressing her tears. "Yes, I've noticed that. He looks a different man, beaten somehow."

"What will you do now, Miss Marion?"

"I love Laurel Manor, and I want to live there someday. If it is the last thing I'll ever do, I'll find a way to get the estate back."

CHAPTER

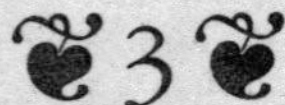

MRS. HALSEY HAD NO COMMENT TO THAT, AND SHE STARED WITH worry at the tight-lipped girl beside her. Miss Marion's tears glittered on her eyelashes, the emerald of her eyes glowing angrily in her thin, pale face. The high spirits, the laughter that was never far from those eyes, were gone, replaced by a sudden maturity and bitterness.

"I knew Papa was devastated by Mother's death, but that he would stoop to the bottle . . . I never thought! He must have lost Laurel Manor while in a drunken haze."

Mrs. Halsey nodded. "You're probably right about that. Brandy was never far from your father's side. Now, however, the doctor has forbidden him to drink as much as a glass of cordial."

"Serves him right," Marion muttered. "How shall I find the strength to forgive him?"

Mrs. Halsey patted her hand. "You will in time, Miss Marion. Don't let bitterness destroy your enthusiasm and high good humor."

Marion dried her eyes on the back of her hand. "Aunt Adele calls my high good humor hoydenish. She says I'm like an untamed pony."

Mrs. Halsey looked away, feeling guilty for agreeing with Miss Marion's aunt. "It's not entirely wrong to be an untamed pony. Charm and candor you have in abundance.'' She sighed. ''It's five years since your mother left this world, and she died too young. She didn't have the time to show you all the ways a young lady needs to know to go on properly in Society. However, your aunt should show you instead of complaining about your lack of decorum.''

''Aunt Adele is always tired.'' A cloud of acute depression settled over Marion as she listened to the housekeeper. Suddenly she found herself in the middle of a nightmare she had no control over. Her father ill and her inheritance gone, she was penniless. It was too dire a dilemma to even think about. She pressed two fingers to her temples as if to force the desperation from her mind. Making herself smile, she hugged Mrs. Halsey. ''Don't you worry about me. I shall find a way to get back the estate.''

Unable to face her father, she walked along the terrace spanning the length of the vast brick house. The majestic Corinthian columns in front of the entrance shone white, and doves cooed on the circular gravel drive as they picked among the pebbles. Birds chirped in the trim box hedges as if nothing had happened. Rothwell Court rested in somnolent calm even if her life had been turned upside down.

In the distance, she could make out the rosy brick facade of her beloved Laurel Manor in the sunny haze. It had the simple but elegant face of the architecture of the past century: tall rectangular windows, embellished iron balconies, and a proud front door. It was a jewel set amidst magnificent gardens, and Marion had longed for the time when she could move into her house. As long as Papa lived at Rothwell Court, she could stay with him, but after what he had done, she didn't want to.

She met Mrs. Halsey in the hallway as she returned half an hour later. The old woman said, ''The new master has offered me to stay, with more pay.'' She wrung her hands.

"If you'd ask him prettily, he might cancel the gambling debt, Miss Marion."

Heatedly, Marion said, "I'd rather die than ask him a favor."

"Really?" sounded Lord Edgewater's dry voice from the library. Marion had not noticed the open door or his shadow on the threshold.

She faced him, anger suffusing her face. "Really! I won't have anything to do with a man who coldheartedly accepts the entire fortune of another man in payment of one night's deep play. What kind of villain are you to do such a thing?" How she disliked him at that moment.

To her surprise, he did not turn from her in wrath. She watched him saunter toward her and offer his arm as if they were about to walk in to dinner. "I believe we have to discuss this in private, Miss Rothwell."

His calmness made her waver. Was she judging him too harshly? Indeed not. The arrogant earl had taken everything from her. Ignoring his arm, she walked stiffly before him, her head held high.

The morning had come with brilliant sunshine only to be dulled by a sudden rainshower. They stood by the tall French doors in the drawing room, watching the rivers of water on the panes. Marion chose to look outside rather than having to face Edgewater's calm gaze.

"I suppose there is no use trying to persuade you to accept Laurel Manor as a gift," he began and slid a finger along the velvet riband of his quizzing glass. "You are very proud for one so young, Miss Rothwell."

When she didn't answer he continued. "It would be a relief if you would accept my offer. I have no time to take care of the estate."

Folding her arms across her middle, Marion glared at him. "You speak of Laurel Manor as a tedious burden, milord, and still you took it without qualms from a man in a desperate gamble. If you were half the gentleman you claim to be, you should have refused to accept the bet.''

The mask of boredom lay heavily on his handsome features. ''I cannot blame you for not knowing the rules of gambling, Miss Rothwell, but I assure you that Sir Horace had a choice to back out of the game before it was too late.''

Lord Edgewater's gaze rested coolly on her. Marion swallowed convulsively, impressed against her will by his calm confidence. Instead of seeing the ruthless gambler, she was aware of his strength, his wide shoulders, his long, well-formed legs. She fantasized about his strong fingers cupping her neck, the taste of his lips—although she had never been kissed before.

He continued, ''As I said, you would be doing me a great favor—''

Marion found her voice at last, husky with emotion. ''I don't want alms from you, Lord Edgewater. But I swear that no later than one year from today, I will be the owner of Laurel Manor once again.''

He looked at her with new interest. ''And how do you plan to go about it?''

''You will find out when the time comes'' was her haughty reply. She had no idea how to go about getting back her inheritance, but she refused to let him see her uncertainty.

He flung out his arms. ''Yesterday, such innocence—today, such age-old female wiles! Should I quaver in my boots?''

Her eyes narrowed. ''You have no right to mock me, milord.'' On those words, she swirled around, almost missing the gleam in his eyes and the ghost of a smile playing over his lips.

''We will meet again'' were her parting words.

Marion hurried upstairs on strangely weak legs to pack, and before half an hour had passed she stood in the hallway once more. She would have to face her father sometime and decided that she couldn't put it off any longer.

Sitting in his Bath chair, Sir Horace was in the garden, in the rose arbor that her mother had planted while she was alive. A graceful white-painted trellis arch supported a vigorous climbing rosebush at the entrance. Papa looked so much older, and so frail, dozing in the shade of a gently swaying maple at the edge of the rose garden. Marion's throat tightened as she stood very still, watching him as if she'd never seen him before. It was as if, overnight, she had become the parent, and he the child.

"Papa?" she called out with a catch in her voice.

His head lifted slowly, and she could see the deep lines of sorrow on his face. As she knelt beside him, she could no longer be angry with him. She hugged him, and he leaned his forehead heavily on her shoulder. "I never thought it would come to this," he muttered. "I was mad that night when I played cards with Lord Edgewater."

"You went to London and didn't visit me?"

He shook his head. "Lord Dunstan had a shooting party at his lodge, and both Edgewater and I attended. That was two weeks ago."

"You had the attack after you lost the gamble?"

He nodded, and as he straightened up she noticed the tears rolling down his cheeks. The attack had left half of his face slightly slack, and his mind seemed distant, as if he was gazing at a different world. "I don't deserve anything but your scorn."

"Be that as it may, but it won't change anything."

He clutched her arm. "Edgewater is a reasonable fellow. Not everyone would offer to cancel the debt."

Bristling with resentment, she stood. "I told him in no

uncertain terms that I won't take alms from him. Why, I wouldn't be able to hold my head up in Society if the gossipmongers got hold of that tidbit."

"I understand." Sir Horace's hands trembled as he indicated the lovely rose garden. "I feel close to your mother here, Marion. I would want to go in peace—right here in this spot where she used to sit and embroider." He glanced at Marion with difficulty, as if his neck was too stiff to move. "Do you remember that, Marion? She was never without her embroidery frame."

"Yes, I remember," Marion said, wiping the tears from her cheeks.

"Sara . . ." he glanced sharply at Marion. "Sara? Is that you? Have you come . . . come to fetch me?"

"No, Papa." Fear clutched at Marion's heart as she realized that her father's mind was wandering. She watched him as he mumbled to himself. After a while, he seemed to come out of a dream. He looked at her with a start. "Where am I, Marion?"

"At home, Papa."

"I . . . don't recall . . ."

"Oh, Papa!" Hugging his frail body to her, she pondered telling him about her decision to somehow get Laurel Manor back but decided against it. If she failed, he would be so disappointed. No use raising his hopes, she thought gloomily.

His voice grew a little stronger. "I hope you might reconsider marrying Sir Cedric. He comes from a distinguished family, and his father was a close friend of mine. I would like to see you settled. He's poor, I admit that, but married to him, you will never lack for anything." His voice trailed off. "You can . . . always live at Laurel Manor."

She wanted instantly to dash his hopes, but her usual aplomb had deserted her. "I . . . I don't know, Papa.

However, I will return to London and finish the Season. You never know what might happen.''

''I'm glad you get to meet young people, darling. I'm afraid I neglected your education in ladylike behavior. I never was any good at childrearing.''

Marion swallowed hard and clutched his hand. ''I shall not disappoint you, Papa.''

He peered at her, his faded eyes embedded in tired lines. ''If you marry Sir Cedric promptly, you don't have to be a financial burden to the Winthrops. Laurel Manor awaits you.''

He has forgotten everything. ''I shall think about it,'' she hedged, gently disentangling her hand from his grip. ''And now I must go. Mrs. Halsey will take good care of you, Papa, until I return.''

She was startled as Lord Edgewater called out behind her. ''I couldn't help but overhear the last of your conversation,'' he said. He smiled, and Marion felt uncomfortable under his candid stare. He continued, ''I've been thinking since you left me in the drawing room, Miss Rothwell. I have a proposition to make.'' Swinging his quizzing glass, he stood in front of Sir Horace. ''I would like to ask for your daughter's hand in marriage,'' he said.

Marion gasped, and Sir Horace straightened. He gave the young man a penetrating stare. ''Are you serious?''

''Papa! Don't listen to him. I will *never* marry him.'' Marion was about to stalk away when Lord Edgewater gripped her arm. Taken by surprise, she waited. He took her hand, caressing her fingers provocatively.

''I'm singularly tired of all the schemes that matchmaking mamas concoct to bring me to the altar. This will strictly be a marriage of convenience, and the estate will go back to you.''

Marion snatched her hand away. Convenience, bah! The

overbearing snake in the grass. Why choose her shoulders on which to unburden his bachelorhood. She clenched her fists. "I will—"

Sir Horace interrupted her. "It's a good idea. Marion, think about it. Our problems would be solved, and you wouldn't have to marry Sir Cedric—if you don't want to."

A new light shone in his eyes, and Marion was loath to dash his hopes. A lump formed in her throat. "I'm not a horse for sale," she said and turned away so that he couldn't see the tears in her eyes. She stared unseeing at the rosebushes.

"Dearest daughter, I know that, but I'm sure the earl will keep you in style. Won't you, Edgewater?"

"Of course I will," said the earl, sounding infinitely bored. "I think that she—she alone—can manage Laurel Manor splendidly."

Marion wanted to kick him in the leg. "I'm not a bargaining tool." She regretted her harsh words when her father's face fell. He looked so pale and ill, and she couldn't bear to see his disappointment. For his sake, she would pretend.

"Oh, every well, Papa. I accept, but on one condition." She glared at Lord Edgewater's inscrutable face. "I want time to get used to the idea, so we won't put the announcement into the papers until the end of the Season." Her eyes challenged the earl to argue her point. He merely shrugged, evidently indifferent as to the outcome of the deal.

"That's a fair request," said Sir Horace. "I'm glad that you're so sensible, Marion."

She nodded curtly. "I shall return to London now." She kissed her father's brow, watching as Lord Edgewater sauntered up the path as unperturbed as if he'd only discussed the weather. The worm!

She caught up with him by the arching trellis. "You listen

to me, Lord Edgewater,'' she said in low tones so that her father couldn't hear her.

''Why do you look so angry? I think it's a good bargain,'' he said.

''For you perhaps. Well, let me tell you, when I have regained the ownership of Laurel Manor, the engagement is annulled. Do you understand?'' She was so angry that she trembled.

A chiding smile played over his face. ''By thunder, you still believe that you'll find a way to retrieve ownership. That's nonsense, my dear.''

Such rage overcame her that she tried to slap him, but he caught her hand in mid air. He pressed a kiss to her fingertips. ''Darling,'' he drawled, ''this is *not* the right way to start a courtship.''

''All you want is to use me as caretaker for Laurel Manor. You don't care about marriage. You don't care about me.''

He chuckled. ''But, Marion, you can't expect my tender feelings after such a short acquaintance.''

She struggled to free her hand from his grip. ''When we return to London, *I don't know you,* is that understood? I don't want anything to do with you.''

''Fair is fair, but I'll have my whole life to get to know you—after we're married.''

''I'd rather marry Sir Cedric,'' she shouted over her shoulder as she marched up the terrace steps. ''I'd rather marry a *toad!*''

His laugh followed her through the house, and she was so mad she thought she would burst. She would show him!

The earl watched her back bristle with anger as she strode the length of the terrace. He'd never met a lady with so hot a temperament. She was dashed entertaining! The females he knew had from childhood been urged to keep their tempers at bay and always act soft and yielding in the company of gentlemen. The earl rubbed his cheek in thought. Maybe it was a mistake to subdue a wild spirit. So many of the ladies he knew were false and calculating, and he never knew whom to trust. He recognized the complete honesty of Marion Rothwell, and he felt an urgent need to pursue her into the house. But no, he'd better not.

He sighed, feeling the lack of sleep heavy in his limbs. She would only ignore him, or hurl more abuses at him. He didn't mind those, but still he didn't want her to be angry with him. Loath to run into Marion as she prepared to leave, he walked into the formal garden at the back of the house. He barely noticed the orderly box hedges and flower borders as tumultuous thoughts filled him.

Every step was burdened with fatigue as he followed the raked paths. He couldn't remember when last he'd slept. Three nights, four nights ago? He had hoped that by exhausting himself on the road he would finally gain the desired rest, but it wasn't to be.

"Dammit, I wish I could lie down and just close my eyes . . ." he muttered under his breath. He shot a longing glance at a hard wrought-iron bench. Any surface would do, anything at all as long as he could go to sleep. Feeling lonely and depressed, he sank down on the bench and glanced at the magnificent facade of Rothwell Court. The wide expanse of brick, the slate roof with its many chimney pots and dormer windows, reminded him of Litton Place. A large house like this could be the loneliest place in the world, he reflected. He thought he saw movement in one of the many windows on the second floor, but he wasn't sure.

Perhaps Miss Rothwell was aiming a rifle at his head from behind the safety of a velvet curtain. One could never be certain what she would do next. At the moment, it was the only thing he was looking forward to finding out.

He sat down and braced his elbows against his knees. Propping chin against one hand, he stared into the distance. In this sunny, quiet spot, he realized how tightly wound up he was inside. If only he could sleep . . . His head seemed to be filled with slow-moving syrup these days. What in the world had induced him to ask for Miss Rothwell's hand in marriage? Had his mind gone so completely mad that he would offer his name to some stranger on the spur of the moment? Something stirred deep inside him, and he realized it was his instinct, his common sense. Perhaps it hadn't been completely idiotic, but only time would tell. S'faith, it'd been a long time since he'd done anything this foolish. Now he had to continue the courting game till God knows when . . .

CHAPTER 4

"MRS. HALSEY, I'M LEAVING," MARION SAID, "AND YOU CAN'T convince me to stay. This isn't my home any longer."

The old woman wrung her hands. "I never dreamed I would live to see this!"

"Your future will be safe here until I return, Mrs. Halsey."

"Miss Marion, if you'd ask the earl prettily, he might cancel the debt. Do it for your father if for no one else."

Heatedly, Marion said, "I'd rather die than ask Lord Edgewater for a favor, and as for Father, he created this problem. Somehow I will correct it, but it won't be easy."

Mrs. Halsey tortured one corner of her white apron between her hands. "I wish you would reconsider, miss. You have . . . er, nothing now. Where will you go? What will you do?"

"I daresay Uncle Bertram and Aunt Adele won't throw me out on the street." In an undertone Marion said to herself, "Though life in the streets might be better than spending the summer with them." She hugged the old housekeeper. "You take good care of Papa until I return."

"God bless you, Miss Marion."

After settling Prinny in his cage on the seat beside her, Marion waved through the window as the Rothwell coach left the estate, passing the earl's curricle as it waited by the door for him to emerge from the house.

Marion gave it a glare, as she now loathed anything connected with the earl.

Everyone had insisted that she bring the Rothwell carriage to London properly chaperoned by her new maid, Pansy, an unassuming country miss with blond braids and a plump bosom. Two grooms rode beside the coach, but she would dismiss them as soon as may be. She had accepted the arrangement without so much as one small argument, but just as soon as they reached Bath, she would send Pansy and the coach back. She fully intended to take the next stage to London. She longed for another fling of adventure before she would be immured by the strict rules of Society.

As the carriage halted in front of the stagecoach office, she informed Pansy of her decision. The maid wailed in despair, "Don't send me back, miss! I promised Mrs. Halsey that I'd look after you." Tears started pouring from her blue eyes and down her ruddy cheeks.

Marion frowned. Tears always made her uneasy since she rarely cried herself. "And what would she do if you return home?"

"She would flay me alive, miss. She's my aunt, and she expects me to do well in your service."

"Hmmm." Marion pursed her lips. "Are you skilled at mending clothes and arranging hair?" When Pansy nodded, she continued, "Where did you learn those skills?"

Pansy shifted her weight to her other foot. "I—I didn't, but I can learn right quickly, miss. Mrs. H. taught me to sew a neat seam."

"Oh, very well. Come along then," Marion said in defeat. "It might be enjoyable to see a friendly face from Burnham every morning instead of Aunt Adele's supercilious abigail. But mind you, I won't be able to pay you much.''

''I don't care, miss.'' Pansy's eyes shone. ''I can't wait to see London.''

''You'll be sorely disappointed, I'm afraid.'' Marion had better luck dismissing the young, inexperienced grooms, who had no desire to visit London. At the glimmer of a coin, they were ready to do her bidding.

On the stage to London, Prinny attracted attention to himself by displaying his vulgar vocabulary to the amusement of some passengers. After receiving a quelling glance from a fat man in the corner of the coach, Marion turned scarlet with mortification.

''A regular sailor, the bird.''

Marion's gaze flew to the owner of the voice, a youngish lady on the opposite seat with mischievous brown eyes. Her blond hair was partly hidden under a straw bonnet with a curling ostrich feather of the same gray color as her elegant traveling costume. This was perhaps a clergyman's wife or a widow of some means, Marion thought. Yet not wealthy enough to own her own carriage. The lady gave a silvery laugh. ''Is he for sale?''

Marion's mouth fell open with surprise. ''N-no, I would think his manners would be appalling to your sensibilities.''

''I find him vastly entertaining,'' the lady replied with another peal of laughter, and she received a full ration of withering stares from the other passengers. She didn't seem to mind.

Marion's curiosity knew no bounds. Too bad Pansy had an outside seat or she would have enjoyed the encounter.

The coach soon halted with creaking brakes at a roadside tavern. As soon as the travelers had alighted, the lady placed a begloved hand on Marion's arm.

"If you don't mind, I would enjoy your company. They serve excellent if plain fare here."

Marion immediately thought of her straitened circumstances and reluctantly accepted the invitation. They found a table in a corner of the taproom. Marion placed Prinny's cage on a chair nearby, and his raucous noises under the cloth drew curious stares from the locals drinking ale at the bar.

"I believe you are as curious about me as I am about you, Miss—"

"Marion Rothwell." Marion met the older woman's scrutiny frankly.

"I'm Mrs. Amelia Milford, an officer's widow from Bath. I lost my husband during the Peninsular campaign."

"I'm sorry," Marion said. "I'm traveling with my maid back to London." Unsure about how much to reveal about herself, she fell silent.

"I'm delighted to have found such refreshing traveling companions." Mrs. Milford pointed toward the cage. "I've never had a parrot as a pet. I have a cat, but he's still in Bath."

"Are you going to London?" Marion dared to ask, trying not to appear too curious.

"Yes. It's lonely in Bath. Most of the patrons of the Pump Room are over fifty years of age, and I'd like some younger company. My brother is traveling abroad, and he offered me the use of his town house in London during his absence. I haven't been to London since my husband died three years ago, so I'm planning to enjoy myself." She gave Marion a penetrating stare. "If my eyes don't deceive me, you're a young lady of Quality," Mrs. Milford added with a smile.

Marion could not help but like the lady with the kind eyes. Mrs. Milford had a vitality that the girls her own age lacked, and Marion found in the older lady a kindred soul.

"If my father knew that I'm traveling via public transportation, he would surely have another apoplexy. I don't wish that on him, but I would much rather see something of the world than merely the interior of his stuffy carriage. Besides, I like the idea of speaking with someone other than toad-faced dullards and peevish dowagers that await me in London." She blushed and looked down at the rough table.

"I don't mean to complain, but my time in London was unpleasant, and now I have to go back there. You see, my uncle doesn't like me, and my aunt always says what he tells her to say. I abhor such weakness in a female, and she always puts on fainting spells to draw attention to herself." She fixed Mrs. Milford with a probing stare. "I daresay you don't suffer from Spasms."

Mrs. Milford laughed. "I should hope not! A most boring pastime."

"My aunt is an expert at fainting, especially when she doesn't get her own way."

"How very tedious to be sure!" Mrs. Milford tapped her fingertips on the table top. "You're going to London to find a husband this Season?"

Heat rose in Marion's cheeks. "That's the rule, but I don't want to get married. Father says I have to wed Sir Cedric Longpole, but I know that all he wants is to marry my . . . fortune." She didn't mention that the fortune was lost or that she might have to tie the knot with the Earl of Edgewater in the end. "I can't abide Sir Cedric. Have you ever met a person with *slimy* eyes? Well, that's how to best describe him."

Mrs. Milford's eye twinkled. "To get leg-shackled to such a person would be a horrid fate indeed." She glanced at the cage. "Perhaps you can convince Sir Cedric that he'll hate your bird."

''No, Sir Cedric is delighted with Prinny.'' She patted the cage and the parrot squawked. ''Just in one day, Prinny learned to imitate Sir Cedric's lisping voice to perfection, and Sir Cedric was awfully impressed. He would be; he only thinks of himself. Then there's this other suitor trying to force himself on me, but I won't have *him.*''

The heavy pain in Marion's chest that she'd subdued since the moment she'd found out her father had gambled away Laurel Manor grew until her eyes swam with tears. She hated herself for showing such weakness in front of a stranger. Mrs. Milford's sympathetic pat on the hand made her lose control, and all the dammed-up sorrow came pouring out, all except the name of Laurel Manor's new owner.

''I'm sorry,'' Marion said with a hiccup. ''I'm usually not a watering pot.''

While Marion dried her eyes, a deep crease of concern formed between Mrs. Milford's eyebrows. ''There is enough sadness for all of us,'' she murmured, the warmth of compassion radiating from her. ''Don't apologize. I understand your sorrow.''

''It's weak to cry,'' Marion said angrily and dashed away another tear. ''It doesn't make things better.''

''Don't worry your head about that, Miss Rothwell. You don't always have to be strong. We aren't impervious to heartache by any means.''

''I shouldn't be pouring out my sorrows.'' Marion watched as the maid placed bowls of onion soup and crusty rolls before her.

''It's often easier to confide one's misfortunes to a stranger. Your confidence will be safe with me. My lips are sealed.''

In companionable silence they took part in the repast, and for the remainder of the meal, Mrs. Milford told Marion stories about her life before her husband died. According to her, London could be fun. There was the theater, the opera, and nights of gambling.

''I loathe gambling,'' Marion said heatedly. ''My father is an inveterate gambler, but I daresay he won't gamble again.''

''For some it's a disease. They *have to* gamble. I, however, gamble just to meet new people, make new friends.''

''You know all the types of cardplay then? I don't know any.''

Mrs. Milford finished her soup. ''I know *vingt-et-un,* basset, silver loo, piquet . . .''

Marion's head jerked up. ''Piquet?''

Mrs. Milford nodded. ''Yes, and without meaning to brag, I must say I'm rather adept at it.''

Marion had never heard anyone extol their luck at the gaming tables with pride. Mrs. Milford had won her admiration. The older woman sparkled with life; she was very different from Marion's dull relatives, and she had shown Marion kindness. Ever since Marion had arrived in London earlier in the spring she'd had precious little of that.

''I think it's time to go,'' Mrs. Milford said and paid for their meal. She had a confidence that Marion envied.

As they left the inn, Marion said, ''I wish I could have a life like yours. No one dictates what you should do or not do.''

Sorrow filled Mrs. Milford's eyes. ''I'd rather that my husband, Charles, were alive. We were happy together, and now I have to look after everything myself. His was a solid shoulder to lean on, and I miss him sorely.''

''I wouldn't want to lean on anyone,'' Marion said and dragged Prinny's cage onto her lap in the coach.

Amelia Milford smiled sadly. ''You don't know what

you're talking about. Independence is all and well. As a widow, no one berates me for traveling on my own, but I'd rather have my husband back."

They silenced in thought as the rest of the passengers climbed inside.

Arriving in London, Marion felt considerably lighter in spirit, thanks to Mrs. Milford. They parted with a promise that they would keep in touch. With one of her mischievous smiles, Amelia gave Marion her card. "Do bring Prinny for a visit sometime."

The Winthrops scolded her as she returned to Albemarle Street with Pansy in tow, carrying cage and portmanteau.

"Really, Marion! Running away in the middle of the night. How could you do anything so cork-brained? It brought on one of my Spasms," Lady Winthrop wailed. Clutching a vinaigrette in one hand and a fan in the other, she reclined like a frail black butterfly on her favorite chaise lounge in her rose and gold boudoir. Even though it was quite warm in the house, a light shawl covered her legs and another her shoulders.

"It gave us all quite a turn to find your note explaining that you had left London. Don't you know how dangerous it is to frequent the streets at night?" berated Sir Bertram, leveling a fierce stare at the culprit standing in the middle of the room.

"I wore . . . Melvin's clothes. I thought it would be easier for a man to travel on the stage."

"I knew it!" cried Melvin Winthrop, his voice full of injury. "My buff pantaloons and my new bottlegreen coat." He clutched his head theatrically, heedless of the chaos he wrought to his carefully arranged curls.

Full of scorn, Marion glared at him. "I will restore your belongings to you in a trice, and no worse for wear." She had quite forgotten the stains from her fall on the street. Refraining to inform them of her night encounter with Lord Edgewater two days past, she addressed Sir Bertram in a frank voice.

"Uncle Bertram, please don't think that I don't appreciate your hospitality, especially now that Father was struck down by illness, but don't make an issue of this. After all, I worried awfully about Father's health, and I knew you would have forbidden me to visit him alone. I could hardly expect you to drop all your engagements and accompany me into the country." She turned to Aunt Adele. "Nor could I expect my dear aunt to travel in her unpredictable state of health." Marion hated to play the role of obedient, grateful niece since she knew they detested her presence in the house. To them she was nothing but an unwanted burden, and she would have to grovel to remain under Uncle Bertram's wing; otherwise they might send her back to her father. If that happened, she would lose her chance to somehow get Laurel Manor back. Buried in the country, she would miss the opportunity to keep a close eye on the earl and whatever new tricks he had in store.

First, she would have to convince her relatives that they had to let her stay for the duration of the Season, a goal that might be difficult to accomplish in her now-impoverished state. With no prospects to offer hopeful suitors to her hand, they would fear she would remain a burden for a long time. She well understood their dilemma.

Marion donned her most innocent mien. "I'm deeply grateful for what you've done for me, Uncle Bertram, but something has happened that might press you into asking me to leave."

Her uncle's eyes narrowed with suspicion. "What now? What have you done?"

Marion forced out a smile. "Nothing. Nothing at all. It's

not me, it's Father. I beg you to listen to my problem.'' To their shocked faces, she proceeded to tell them the cause of her sudden lack of fortune. ''Father gambled away the entire estate. Aside from the clothes I wear, I have nothing left.''

Aunt Adele suffered another Spasm, something quite unnecessary in Marion's opinion. She needed her aunt's support. Melvin paced the floor with small mincing steps, huffing into his shirtpoints. While Marion vigorously fanned her aunt's face, she studied Uncle Bertram's bull-like features. Why did she find him so unpleasant? She never felt comfortable in his company. He always *loomed* over her, complaints falling readily from his lips. How Aunt Adele had found any trait worth admiring in the man was beyond her. But then Aunt Adele hadn't had much choice. She had married Sir Bertram when everybody expected her to remain a spinster. He'd probably married her for her money.

Sir Bertram trod back and forth on the costly Aubusson carpet. ''Oh dear . . . oh dear!'' He stopped in front of Marion, his face stern. ''Is this true, or is it one of your silly jokes, young miss?''

''Of course not, Uncle. Lord Edgewater is now the owner of Laurel Manor.''

Her aunt showed sudden signs of recovering from her feigned fainting spell. She opened one eye. ''The Earl of Edgewater?'' She heaved herself to an upright position on the chaise lounge. ''Marion, are you implying that you've met the *Earl of Edgewater*?''

Marion sank onto the nearest chair. ''Yes, and how fervently I wish I never had.'' She chewed on her bottom lip, reliving the hours in his lordship's company. Chagrined, she had to admit to herself that she had enjoyed his company immensely—until the moment she found out the truth about his "dull business trip."

Her aunt's eyes shone with a strange gleam. "Who would ever have thought that Pierce Litton favored such deep cardplay? The rumors, however, say he's quite the gambler."

Sir Bertram snorted. "It doesn't signify in the least. The young bucks are forever gambling and hanging around low taverns drinking Blue Ruin. That's when they are not betting on some cockfight or other. No, in my heyday, things were different."

"Ha! I know a man who lost ten thousand pounds during one sitting at White's twenty years ago," Lady Winthrop said cuttingly.

Sir Bertram made a movement of impatience. "That was very different!" he snorted. "*I* never wagered my estate, and I don't understand how your brother Horace could have done such a maggot-witted thing."

Aunt Adele bristled. "My brother wouldn't do such a thing without a solid reason, I'm sure." But her voice held little conviction. "Of course, we don't know the whole story, and perhaps we never will, since my poor brother is in such a feeble condition," she added with dying airs.

Marion choked on a wave of hot tears and stood unsteadily. During their bickering, her guardian had quite forgotten her predicament. "The Earl of Edgewater is as much to blame as my father. No one in his right mind would confiscate an entire estate at the turn of a playing card."

"Hmmm." Sir Bertram rubbed his triple chin as he pondered her words. "You're in somewhat of a pickle, m'dear."

"Are you going to send me back home?" Marion wrung her hands in theatrical fashion, hoping to play on his sympathy. She didn't particularly like to pretend an eagerness to stay with them that she didn't feel, but more than Sir Bertram's likes and dislikes hung in the balance. It was imperative that he let her stay for the duration of the Season. "I couldn't bear the thought of being a burden to you, dear Uncle." She accompanied her words with a troubled smile.

Three pairs of eyes stared at her suspiciously.

"Dear Marion, you would never be a burden. However, we might have to send you back. How will you ever find a husband without a dowry?" Aunt Adele began. "Besides, I distinctly heard you say upon several occasions that you dislike London."

"I might have to find some kind of employment to support myself once Father's ready funds run out. As you well know, most of his assets are tied up in Rothwell Court."

"Hmm, seems that you know a lot about your father's affairs," Sir Bertram muttered.

"He had a habit of confiding in me when I lived at home." Marion's back was rigid. "I take it you will not stop me from seeking work?"

"Work? How can you speak about employment, Marion?" Aunt Adele puffed herself up with outrage. "I have never heard such a preposterous idea. You're a lady of Quality, and as such you shall not soil your hands with toil. I won't stand for it!"

"I might not have a choice."

Calculation filled Lady Winthrop's eyes as she said, "You have always made yourself very useful in the library here by helping Bertie restore order to the books."

"Yes, that's a solution, for the time being, Marion. I know I can count on you for a few hours every morning," Sir Bertram said, "and we shall speak no more about your misfortune."

Marion listened to the underlying request that she ought to make herself useful in the future if she wanted to stay. Her status had dropped from heiress to poor relation, and now she could expect to be ordered about. But at least she could stay.

A brilliant plan had dawned on her, and she longed to return to her room and ponder the possibilities. Meekly she said, "I'm exceedingly grateful for your hospitality. You shan't regret it. By the end of the Season, your books will be cataloged and cross-indexed, Uncle Bertram." She turned to her aunt. "I sew a very neat stitch, and it would be a pleasure to help you in any way possible," she said, crossing her fingers behind her back as she lied about her sewing skills. "I daresay I won't go out much at night since no gentleman has shown much interest in my company."

"Well, you must accept any invitation, and there is always Sir Cedric." Aunt Adele sent Uncle Bertram an excited glance. "As we informed you earlier, we wouldn't be averse to an instant, *quiet*—have to think about the cost, you know—wedding to him. Society would understand such haste in your straitened circumstances."

The wind had suddenly shifted. A forceful invisible hand pushed Marion toward the horrifying prospect of marrying Sir Cedric, but she knew to hold her tongue even though she bristled with outrage. "Though I appreciate your thoughtfulness on my behalf, I cannot in all earnest say that I like Sir Cedric."

Sir Bertram waved a dismissing hand. "You have no say in the matter, Marion. You must let us decide about your future. After all, we have vastly more experience of such matters."

"You must realize you're lucky that anyone is willing to

wed you,'' Melvin said and touched a curl of her hair with revulsion.

''Desist, Melvin. That was a very unkind thing to say,'' admonished Aunt Adele.

Marion dreamed of ways to pull out Melvin's fingernails slowly, but instead she gave him a bland smile. ''May I go to my room now?'' she asked, and her uncle nodded his consent.

As she left the salon, Melvin cried, ''Don't forget to return my clothes—in mint condition. Or I shall have your hide.''

''Worm,'' Marion said *sotto voce* as she closed the door behind her.

The interview with her relatives had gone the way she expected. She could stay as long as she kept making herself useful. Marion grimaced with dismay as she lay on her bed, her hands behind her head. She stared at the ceiling where a plaster angel holding a garland mocked her. If she did not wish to see herself wed to Sir Cedric within a month, she had better execute the idea that had come to her earlier. She had no other choice.

Pansy had unpacked all her things, but there was no hide nor hair of her maid.

Looking at the watch pinned to her dress, Marion knew this would be the best time to sneak out of the house. Her aunt would be taking a nap and Sir Bertram spent every afternoon at White's. They need not know where she had gone, nor would they care. By bringing along her maid, she would show the decorum expected of her as she went into the city.

She had pulled on a pale blue spencer with a matching bonnet as Pansy returned. The country maid chattered excitedly about the impressions of her first day in London.

She barely paused to let Marion issue the order that they were going to take a walk.

Pansy didn't need asking twice. Together they went into the sunshine of the afternoon. "Where are we going?"

"We're going to visit the lady we met on the stage-coach."

Set on the promise she had given Lord Edgewater, she would make every effort to regain Laurel Manor. She prayed that Amelia Milford would help her.

CHAPTER

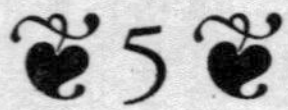

"THIS WAY, MISS ROTHWELL. MRS. MILFORD IS ENTERTAINING A visitor in the blue salon," an unexpectedly muscular butler informed Marion as she presented her card.

As Pansy waited obediently on the bench right inside the door, Marion followed the broad-shouldered man across the dark-paneled foyer whose only adornment was a shiny medieval armor in one corner and a series of gloomy portraits in gilt frames. Amelia evidently hadn't yet had time to add any female touches to her brother's town house. Marion recognized her friend's silvery laugh as the butler opened a door at the end of a small corridor off the hallway.

"Miss Marion Rothwell," he announced.

"Thank you, Smithers," Amelia said as Marion entered the room.

Marion thought Amelia Milford was an excessively handsome woman, tall, well-proportioned, who carried herself with dash. Today she wore a smart morning gown of green muslin trimmed with lace. Marion instantly relaxed under the friendly dark gaze leveled at her. If only she had an ounce of Amelia's self-confidence!

"I suppose you're shocked to see me on your doorstep so quickly after we met, but I have a problem—" Marion noticed a movement in the wing chair partly turned away from the door. As the tall, elegantly dressed man rose and leveled a quizzing glass at her, Marion gasped. "Not you again!"

"Why not?" drawled the Earl of Edgewater. "I didn't have a fatal accident on the Bath road, as you probably wish I'd had." A cynical smile accompanied his pronouncement.

"A pity, indeed," Marion murmured under her breath. He looked as handsome as she remembered, but his skin had an unhealthy pallor, and his eyes were ringed with dark shadows.

Amelia stared curiously from one to the other. "Pierce, I had no idea you knew Miss Rothwell. Where did you meet?"

The earl gave Marion a calculating stare, and she wondered if he would divulge their night ride through London. "Well . . ." he began. "I believe I shall let Miss Marion explain the circumstances." He gave a dry laugh. "I might add that she holds me in very low esteem, so don't be surprised—"

"And you deserve every bit of my scorn," Marion said heatedly. She silenced with a blush as she remembered one of Aunt Adele's lectures of late: Always Appear in a Quiet, Ladylike Manner. Marion shuddered. It was so difficult to remember all the rules, and Father had never told her how to behave. Be yourself and don't hurt anyone was his motto, but True Ladies were *never* themselves.

"It appears you've an abundance of contempt for me," the earl muttered.

Marion gave him a sweet, poisonous smile. "I've every reason not to regard you highly. Why, a snake deserves more respect, should it slither across this floor."

"I say!" He turned to Amelia. "How about that? That's what I call hatred." The earl stepped across the gray-and-blue carpet. "Under the circumstances, I think it's time for me to leave, Amy. I'm sure Miss Marion doesn't want me to overhear as she confides her problems to you.''

He towered over her, and Marion was acutely aware of his manly charms, broad shoulders, the strong, clean-shaven jaw, the hooked nose. His sharp, gray gaze penetrated to her very soul, and her heartbeat escalated. *Something*, an unspoken communication, passed between them, making Marion's knees melt. Behind the face of the ogre that had stolen her inheritance she saw someone else, a very attractive, intriguing man whom she yearned to know better. He snatched up her hand before she had a chance to protest. His skin was cool and his grip strong.

She detested herself as her blush deepened. What did he see? A pinch-faced urchin with a tangled mop of red hair and round spectacles?

''As usual, I find you highly entertaining, not the regular run-of-the-mill young miss,'' he said, and his eyes glowed teasingly as he kissed her fingertips. ''I'm sure I'll see you again in the near future.''

''I certainly hope not!'' she said in an undertone.

She watched as he bent over Amelia and pecked her cheek. If she had known that the earl would be here, she would never have come, Marion thought.

Yet, somehow the day seemed less lustrous after he left the room.

''Well, well, the world is small. I had no idea you knew one of my old friends—or rather one of dear Charles's school chums,'' Amelia said and urged Marion toward the sofa.

''Now tell all about your problem,'' she added as she sat down next to Marion. ''I'd be delighted to help you if I can.''

Marion's gaze flitted around the room, vaguely registering blue velvet draperies with gold-tasseled ties, light blue walls, and blue-and-gold upholstery. Amelia's brother evidently had both taste and wealth. But she wasn't here to admire the interior of the town house.

"I had no idea that you knew the earl," she said and studied Amelia's candid face and kind eyes. "You see, my problem involves him."

"*Really?* This is a surprise. I thought Pierce did everything in his power to stay away from young, unwed misses like yourself."

"Well, he does, but he . . . well, ran into me one evening. I'm sure he wanted nothing to do with me, but, in a manner, I happened to get in his way."

"How intriguing. Pray tell me more."

"You recall that I told you about my misfortunes on the way home from Bath. This will surprise you, but the Earl of Edgewater is the man who won Laurel Manor from my father at that disastrous card game."

Amelia's eyes first widened in surprise, then darkened with distress. "How very tedious. I thought Pierce would not partake in such deep gambling."

"He says he doesn't usually, but the night Father lost the estate was different. I don't know what to believe, and I don't care. My main concern is to retrieve the estate."

A smile spread over Amelia's face. "You show a lot of resolve, Marion. How can I best help you?"

Marion decided to come right to the point. "I'd like to learn to play piquet so well that I could recover my inheritance from the earl in the same way he won it from Father."

"I see. And you believe I could teach you?"

"If anyone, you can, Mrs. Milford. You told me yourself that you're an expert at every conceivable card game." Before the older woman could speak Marion continued, "I don't have much money, but I'm prepared to work for my tuition.'' She indicated the mess on the Queen Anne desk by the window. ''I have excellent skills organizing papers and books, and I'm not averse to working with my hands, although I have little knowledge of cooking and cleaning.''

''Quite an irresistible offer!'' Amelia said, her eyes alight with amusement. ''Your resourcefulness does you credit, but you don't have to pay me. It'll be entertaining to watch you best the earl, who is an excellent card player, I might add.'' Amelia's eyebrows lifted in inquiry. ''Are you sure you want to challenge him?''

Marion, after taking a deep shuddering breath, said, ''I've never wanted anything more. If I don't try, I'll lose Laurel Manor forever, and someone has to try to salvage Papa's pride. He can't do it himself, after the stroke.''

Amelia rose and began pacing the floor. ''I don't know if I'm knowledgeable enough to teach you to beat the earl, but I do admire your spirit. I don't know of any lady in your position who would have chosen such an unusual way to solve a problem.'' She laughed. ''I'm on your side. Edgewater must be made to return your inheritance: that is all there is to it.''

Marion shot her a grateful glance. ''He already offered to do just that, but I won't accept any alms from him.''

''I see.'' Amelia pondered the statement. ''That was decent of him. Your pride has put you in quite a predicament now.'' She returned to her seat and faced Marion. ''It might have been easier to accept his offer.''

Marion was about to tell her new friend about Lord Edgewater's offer of marriage, but that humiliation was too deep to share at this moment. ''As I said, I won't accept charity from him.''

''It's unfortunate that your father had to gamble that night, and for such high stakes.''

''He always liked to gamble, but usually he didn't get

involved too deeply—at first. He should have learned from his mistakes. He had the most awfully bad luck, always losing.''

''Some people take gambling too seriously,'' Amelia said. ''I hope you're not like your father, or I might be to blame if you become addicted.''

''I'm not like Father in that respect. I never had much interest in gambling.'' Marion raised her chin. ''If you have second thoughts, I'll try to find another teacher. I don't want to force you to do this.''

Silence fell for a few moments as Amelia Milford scrutinized her thoughtfully.

''I will teach you how to play piquet. Pierce will probably never forgive me for it, but you must have your chance. I understand that.'' She took Marion's hand and squeezed it. ''Pierce has more than enough wealth. He doesn't need Laurel Manor.''

''He called the lovely estate a tedious burden, you know. I find him overbearing and condescending—that's why I couldn't accept charity from him. I must learn the game to beat him.'' *Then he cannot force me to accept his offensive proposal of marriage,* she added silently.

''Piquet is a strategical game, and you have to play with the avid gamblers to get enough practice. I shall endeavor to invite you to some card evenings here, but I don't know how you'll find a way to attend without the guests spreading rumors about you. As one making her debut in Society, you need a spotless reputation.''

Marion gave Amelia a frank stare. ''I understand that, but I don't care. I only need a good reputation to marry, and I don't really want to get wed.''

Amelia looked surprised. ''Why not? You can't expect your father to provide for you forever. You'll have to marry.''

Marion clasped her hands tightly in her lap. ''Only gentlemen whom I abhor have shown any interest at all in me. One in particular, but I'd rather be dead than to marry him.''

''That bad, is it?''

Marion blinked rapidly. ''Yes . . . that bad. No one wants me for myself. I'm not lovely . . . like you.''

''Surely beauty isn't skin-deep? There's more—''

''*No!* Don't pretend that it's not important—perhaps the most important—''

''That's nonsense,'' Amelia said sharply. ''Attraction comes from within. Why, my Charles was cross-eyed and bald, and I still loved him.''

Marion could not help but laugh. ''Cross-eyed? You must be bamming me.''

Amelia shook her head. ''No. I'll show you a portrait later, and you can see for yourself.''

''I'm glad I made your acquaintance, Mrs. Milford. You seem to be the answer to my problems.''

''Call me Amy.'' The older woman eyed Marion's hair dubiously. ''There's the problem of your hair, if you are to attend one of my card evenings. Someone is bound to recognize you, and I wouldn't want to be blamed for ruining your reputation.''

''I could wear a wig, of a more discreet color.''

Amelia nodded. ''Discretion is the key word here.''

''My hair has been the grief of my life.''

Amy laughed. ''I think it looks very pretty, like a fiery soft halo, but, unfortunately, easily recognizable.''

Marion shuddered. ''A curse rather than a halo. When do we start? When will you teach me piquet?''

''If you're planning to beat Pierce Litton, you'll have to work very hard. Since he's a master of the game, he'll have all the advantage over you. He probably started at your age, and he's twenty-seven now."

"Oh. Well, I'll have to practice night and day."

"Marion, what an unusual girl you are, to be sure!"

"You seem to know Lord Edgewater very well." Marion studied the assured woman beside her.

"Ah! I know everyone. While alive, Charles was quite the Society buck, so we attended many parties. Everybody liked him, and as I said before, Pierce went to school with him. That's how I met Pierce. He's very protective of his friends, and he came here just as soon as he heard that I had arrived to make sure that I had everything I needed."

"Yes . . . but I can't look at him in a favorable light. After all, he's my enemy." Marion rose. "Now I must return to my uncle's house."

"We must make up some excuse for you to come here and learn the card game."

"I'll contrive something."

"Perhaps afternoons would be best."

Marion nodded. "Aunt Adele never leaves her bedroom before noon, then takes long naps in the afternoon. I'm left to my own devices most of the time."

Amelia stood and held out her hand. "Very well, we'll start as soon as may be."

"Tomorrow?" Marion's hope soared.

"How much fun it'll be, Marion . . . It will be worth the effort—if only to see Pierce's long face when he's beaten by—"

"A mere stripling," Marion added.

CHAPTER

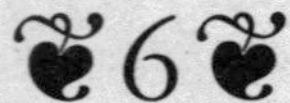

Marion settled into her exciting ''secret'' life, although she hated staying on at Albemarle Street. In the mornings she worked in her uncle's study organizing his books, and at other times she carried and fetched for her aunt, even though Lady Winthrop had a personal maid. Even so, her pin money dwindled into nothing now that her father failed to send her anything. She heard that his mind had deteriorated but that he continued to get stronger physically.

Her uncle evidently felt he had no obligation to pay for her services as his librarian. Marion had to pay Pansy's wages in castoffs and accessories. The maid soon looked as well dressed as herself, which didn't mean much since the gowns were rather threadbare. Though to Pansy, every ''new'' dress was heaven.

Marion only became more determined to hone her skill at the game of piquet. Once she managed to win the estate back, she would leave London and never return. As many afternoons as she could get away, she went to Amelia's house to study the strategies of the card game. She learned that she would have to anticipate her adversary's hand of cards while establishing a strong suit of her own to gain the highest points, and at the same time remember which cards had been played or discarded. She would have to deduce her chances at scoring high in the initial declaring of the cards at hand, then gain as many tricks as the cards were played. She found the feints and tactics challenging and intriguing.

She didn't see Pierce Litton at all during this time, even though she attended some of the social gatherings to please her aunt. The earl didn't attend the same balls and routs, but Sir Cedric Longpole did.

Marion found that Sir Cedric's interest had cooled considerably after hearing the rumors of her loss of fortune. When her father's wild night of gambling became common knowledge, Marion found her status of perennial wallflower becoming ominously fixed. At least she had danced sometimes before, but now—

The balls were a torture to attend, but Marion had to force herself to be agreeable to her aunt when she insisted that Marion do her duty to appear at the various functions.

"You must marry, there's nothing else for it," Aunt Adele said one morning. "How else are you going to live?" That subtle question told Marion that her welcome was limited to Albemarle Street, and that fact gave her a profound feeling of loneliness. However, it also made her relieved; she had no intention of becoming a burden to her relatives. By the end of the Season she would be back home in Somerset with dear Papa.

"I do attend the festivities, Aunt Adele, but no gentleman has paid me special interest. Though I'm not to be blamed, I'm still part of the scandal that involved Papa's desperate gambling. That's one reason why the gentlemen scorn me."

She let her hands lapse on the embroidery frame in her lap. Her aunt had given her the task of finishing a firescreen that she herself had started ten years before and never completed. Marion hated every stitch, but she stubbornly clenched her teeth and continued embroidering rose after rose of the motif. She glanced quickly out the window, where the morning sun shone cheerfully. If only she could ask her aunt to take a stroll in the park and admire the flowers . . . if only.

"I can't imagine why the gentlemen are so partial to blonds," Aunt Adele said and tucked the wool blanket closer around her legs. Reclining on the chaise lounge, she fanned herself languidly while staring with distaste at Marion's unruly red hair.

"Miss Ralston doesn't have any problems attracting suitors," Marion pointed out. Emily Ralston was the toast of the Season, a classical beauty with glorious raven-black hair and eyes the color of sapphires. Marion ought to hate her, but she felt nothing but a vague distaste. All Miss Ralston every cared for were the latest hair styles and gowns from France. She knew the family tree of every eligible bachelor above the rank of baronet, never forgetting to point out that her dear uncle was a marquis, no less. She'd never read a play by Shakespeare—she probably didn't even know who the great playwright was. "Shakespeare?" she would ask and tilt her head in that affected way of hers. "Is he a new fashionable hairdresser?"

Marion chuckled to herself and deliberately made a crooked stitch on the canvas. She could never be like Miss Ralston, and she didn't want to be, even if it meant remaining a wallflower for the rest of her life. This afternoon she would make every effort to learn the last strategies of piquet. The sooner she could leave London, the better. She would leave in triumph, there was no doubt about that. Then it didn't matter that she was ugly as sin.

"You must apply yourself, Marion. No gentleman will look twice at you if you wear that forbidding look on your face. And I've caught you squinting at times."

"Auntie dearest, there are more things to life besides

marriage.'' Marion gave her relative a bland, innocent smile.

''I have yet to hear a more ridiculous statement from you, Marion. I fail to understand your negative attitude toward holy wedlock.''

''In the past, gentlemen like Sir Cedric—who doesn't have a feather to fly with—showed some interest, but now that my inheritance is lost, they shy away from me. In fact, they *run* when they see me coming.''

''If you *applied* yourself to your hair—'' Aunt Adele took a whiff of her vinaigrette bottle tightly clutched in her hand and gave Marion a covert glance.

''I might as well shave my head! Then the gentlemen'll be sure to notice me.''

''Marion, please!'' You give me palpitations with your frank outbursts. It's highly unladylike to criticize the hapless gentlemen. The way you speak, one might think that all of them are fortune hunters of the worst kind. I, for one, know that Sir Cedric had nothing but tender feelings toward you.''

Marion stopped the word ''humbug'' from popping out of her mouth at the last moment. She smiled meekly. ''You're always right, Aunt Adele.'' She stood and packed the embroidery into a wicker basket. ''I must go downstairs and catalog all the books under the letter K this morning. It won't do to get behind on that chore. I must please Uncle Bertram with my dedication.''

Before her aunt could say something to keep her at her sewing, Marion fled out of the morning room.

In no hurry to start on the books, she walked down the curving stairs in a leisurely fashion. She pulled her fingertips along the carved balustrade and wrinkled her nose as her fingers came away grimy with dust. If she owned this lovely town house, she would treasure it forever and not let dust mar its glory.

However, this morning the atmosphere of the house stifled her. She wished more than ever that she could take a stroll in the park. April had moved into May, and the city had taken on a bright, smiling face. Even the muddy Thames glittered on a day like this, she thought, and longed to see it.

With a deep sigh, she headed toward the library at the back of the hallway. Hearing her uncle's booming voice coming from that room, she realized that he wasn't alone. She stopped outside the door. It stood slightly ajar, and when she could clearly hear Sir Cedric's tenor voice issuing an answer to Sir Bertram's request, she instantly found out what that request had been.

"I regret to say that my interest in marrying Miss Marion has cooled. She shows not the least warmth toward me, never has, in fact."

"I'm asking you, Sir Cedric, begging you to reconsider. After all, you asked for her hand not one month ago. You can't go back on that offer now."

"Sir, she turned me down on a number of occasions."

Marion heard her uncle shove some papers aside on his desk, a sure sign of his irritation. "That's neither here nor there. I can't get the chit off my hands, and that a fact! If I'm not careful, she'll remain in this household for the rest of my life, and that's unthinkable."

Marion gasped, and a sensation of utter misery spread through her body, from the area of her heart to the tips of her toes. She stood as if rooted to the floor, unwilling to hear more, yet unable to move away.

"Sir . . . your offer is somewhat unorthodox," Sir Cedric said hesitantly.

Marion knew what her uncle was going to say next, but

she remained, waiting to hear the last of his harsh judgment flow over her like a bucket of icy water.

"I repeat my offer, and you can't refuse, Cedric—not in your current situation. I'll settle ten thousand pounds on you if you wed the girl. Marion won't find another prospect, not in her present circumstances. Even when her inheritance was intact, you were her only serious suitor."

"But times have changed," Sir Cedric whined.

"You don't have the opportunity to choose, my boy. You're poor as a church mouse, and you always will be if you don't take my offer. Besides, you once said you harbored a soft spot for my niece. Was that a lie?"

Marion sensed Sir Cedric's hesitation. She didn't wait to hear another word. She couldn't take another lie, another falsehood. Knowing she was a hopeless prospect, she didn't need to be reminded. But as she hurried away, she heard Sir Cedric say:

"Oh, very well! I accept your bargain."

Marion clasped her hands over her ears and disappeared into the gold salon that was located next door to the library. She quickly closed the door behind her—just in time to hear Sir Bertram entering the hallway with Sir Cedric in tow.

Dazed, she sank down on the sofa in front of the fireplace and stared unseeing at the firescreen of tooled copper. Her uncle's words whirled around and around in her head. She hadn't realized just how much he wanted to get rid of her, how much he loathed her presence. Hot tears swam in her eyes and she tried to swallow, but her throat was constricted with grief. Every inch of her body ached with sadness. At that moment she hated herself, and her ugly red hair, and her spectacles. She pulled them off and hurled them across the room. They landed in a dried flower arrangement on a table by the window. She wished she never had to put them on again, but just as that thought flitted through her mind, she realized that her vision was uncomfortably blurred.

Her next thought was to run from the house and never return. Then they would worry about her. She would throw herself into the river. Yes, that was a way to get rid of the pain. Still, she knew she couldn't do it. Blinking hard against the tears, she struggled desperately to contain her sorrow as it seemed about to engulf her. If she let go, she would end up a tear puddle on the floor, she thought and clenched her hands so hard the nails bit into her palms. She sat quietly erect staring into herself for what seemed an eternity.

She could find no way to reconcile herself with her lack of beauty and grace, but she could try not to think about it. If anything, she ought to push away her uncle's hateful words, she thought while choking down another wave of tears. Don't think about them, act as if nothing has happened, she told herself. You knew all this before, so why is it such a surprise? You knew your uncle resented your presence, didn't you? He never liked you, but what does it matter?

After ten minutes of constant struggle, she managed to gain control over her misery. An icy anger started to rise inside her, and she drew strength from it. Her uncle thought he could sell her off as if she were a piece of furniture, did he? The man evidently had less decency than a common rat, she thought, and stood. Guided by the light from the window, she stumbled across the floor toward the table with the flower arrangement. She fumbled among the brittle twigs and blossoms until she found her spectacles. Thank God they hadn't broken. She pushed them up on her nose and fastened them behind her ears. There was a mirror in a gilt frame above the table, but she refused to look at herself.

She hated the person that stared back at her almost as much as she hated Uncle Bertram.

Taking a deep breath, she walked toward the door. No one would know what she'd overheard, but she would make her uncle pay, and Sir Cedric, too. Uncle had no interest in her—just as the Earl of Edgewater had shown no real interest in her. They earl had only seen a way to stave off match-making mamas and find a manager for Laurel Manor that he'd so inconveniently been saddled with. He probably figured that if he married her, he could leave her at the estate and never bother with her again. To both of them she was nothing but a stepping-stone. Once they had gained their respective goals through her, they would not look at her again.

She peeked into the foyer. No one was there. If she had met her uncle while still in such a turbulent, emotional state, she might have flown at him with knotted fists. Straightening her shoulders and taking several deep breaths, she went into the library and closed the door. She recoiled at the sweet scent of her uncle's hair pomade that still lingered in the air, but she forced herself to get on with her work. While she cataloged the books, she would come up with some ideas for revenge.

The memory of Sir Cedric's face floated in her mind; the sandy hair, the narrow pinched features that weren't totally unacceptable had they been devoid of the virulent pimples and moist lips. He constantly licked his lips, and it made her shudder. His clammy hands were another matter . . . In his presence she always felt that she had to keep an eye on his hands.

If her uncle thought he would get away with selling her off like a sack of potatoes, he was a fool. If he believed she would be overset with gratitude at his plan, he was more of a coxcomb than she'd ever imagined!

CHAPTER 7

"No! For the hundredth time *no*, and anything you say won't change my mind," Marion said to the kneeling Sir Cedric and crossed her arms over her chest.

He rose from his awkward pose. "But you *m-must* marry me," he stuttered. "There's no other way."

Marion simply pinched her lips shut, relieved that she'd been able to hold her temper. Twenty-four hours had passed since she'd overheard her uncle's conversation with Sir Cedric. It had given her plenty of time to gather her strength to face the distasteful proposal when Sir Cedric arrived to "have a private word" with her.

"Do leave, Sir Cedric. I'll never marry you, and you know it. Why keep up this pretense of loving me when, in fact, you don't care a fig for me." She rose from the sofa and went toward the door, Sir Cedric coming after her in a rush.

"I shall tell your uncle about your stubbornness," he threatened.

"Uncle Bertram knows my views on the subject."

"But he doesn't approve of your opinion, and well you know it. He wants us to marry, and since he's your guardian—" Sir Cedric gripped her arm as she was about to exit. He dragged her from the door and into his arms.

Pinning her clumsily against his chest, he tried to kiss her.

"Stop that," she demanded and pushed against him. "Leave me alone."

It was fortunate that Aunt Adele chose that moment to return to the gold salon. Halting in the doorway, she squealed with outrage. "Sir Cedric! Unhand my niece this instant."

With a hangdog expression, the young man complied. Marion drew a breath of relief as his arms fell away from her. She stepped back and glared at him.

"I won't marry him," she told her aunt.

Aunt Adele fluttered her fan in front of her face in agitation and inhaled a whiff of vinaigrette. "Your uncle won't be pleased, not pleased at all. Life will be difficult for all of us when he finds out."

"I shall go and tell him myself."

"He went out of town on business, dear. Won't be back until next week. He expected this to be settled today, and the banns read on Sunday." She gave Marion a forceful glance, but Marion didn't lower her eyes. It was the older woman who yielded.

"Oh, dear. What will Bertram say?" Aunt Adele staggered against the doorframe. "I feel faint."

Sir Cedric hastened to support her, then led her tenderly to the sofa. He settled her among the needlepoint cushions, and Marion spread a shawl over her legs.

"Oh dear, oh dear," wailed Aunt Adele, and Marion went to summon the maid.

"You haven't heard the end of this, Miss Marion," Sir Cedric shouted after her. She shuddered with distaste. She wasn't going to give in to their pressure, she thought, clenching her fists. Somehow she'd find a way to stall the decision until she'd won back Laurel Manor. Thank God,

Uncle Bertram wouldn't return for a week. It gave her time to practice her card skills.

Marion lived for her afternoons with Amelia, who treated her like an equal and never commented condescendingly on her hair or her spectacles. A week after Sir Cedric's proposal, Marion had calmed down enough to think about it with some distance. Uncle Bertram would be back in London any day now, and by then she must have a strategy to present.

"You're quite a good player now, Marion. I think it's about time you got a chance to test your mettle against real gamblers," Amelia said and shuffled the cards. "I know that, innocent maiden that you are, you're not supposed to even know about the existence of such 'vile' places as gaming salons," she added with a wry smile. "Reputation, remember?"

"It's not important," Marion replied. "I don't care what the world will think of me."

"Well, I do," Amelia said and rose from the chair. "We'll endeavor to disguise you. Are you free tonight?"

They had been playing cards in her boudoir, and now she crossed the room and took down a hatbox from the top of her armoire.

"Yes, Sir Cedric came around to ask me if I would accompany him to the opera, but I said I had a sore throat."

"You sound dejected, Marion," Amelia said and pulled a blond wig from the box. "In fact, you haven't smiled for the entire week."

The misery that had squeezed Marion's chest since she'd overheard her uncle's conversation with Sir Cedric prevented her from confiding everything to her friend. As it was too painful to speak about, she bore the humiliation alone.

"What have you there, Amelia?" she asked, changing the subject.

"I thought you'd better hide your lovely curls under this. That way no one will recognize you." She marched her protegée to her dressing table and pushed her down onto the chair.

Marion refused to look at herself in the mirror, but Amelia brushed and pinned her hair close to her skull, then slid the wig over her head.

"There! You look very different."

Marion took a peek at her image, and her eyes widened in awe. "What lovely hair," she said. "I wish—" She halted her tongue. It was no use complaining to Amelia.

"Tonight I'll pretend that I'm somebody else," Marion said and fluffed out the long blond curls of the wig. Her spirits rose accordingly, "Where are we going?"

"To the Gold Room in St. James's."

Marion gasped. "St. James's? No *lady* ever goes there."

Amelia's lips quirked at the corners. "Well, perhaps some . . . those considered *fast.* Those who don't want to be recognized wear half-masks."

"Aunt Adele would surely have a double Spasm if she got wind of this."

Amelia frowned and pressed her fingertips to her temples. "I'll be to blame if anything happens to you there. Oh, dear, what have I gotten myself into?"

"I'll go even if you don't," Marion said, raising her chin.

"That's the problem. You're too stubborn for your own good." Amelia sighed, then rose. "Wear something simple, Marion, a dress that no one will notice later."

"That kind of dress is the only type I've got. My relatives don't believe in the latest fashions from France, or anywhere else—not for me anyway." She made her voice cheerful. "When are we leaving?"

"Be here at eleven sharp. I'll send my brother's carriage for you. It'll wait at the corner of Grafton and Albemarle."

Marion's introduction to the gaming rooms went quite smoothly, though the thick tobacco smoke made her eyes water. As they entered the main room, she suffered from a feeling of acute awkwardness. She feared her new blond wig would fall off and that every guest would recognize her immediately. Young blades acted too familiar with her, squeezing her arms and breathing down her decolletage, but Amelia was close at hand to fob off overly ardent admirers.

Miss Milo Brown was the name Amelia had invented for her at the spur of the moment—should someone inquire. Some did, to Marion's surprise. Some young gentlemen gave her approving glances. Such success was heady after all the rejection at the Society balls. Amelia wore a wig and mask, since she wanted no rumors to be spread about her. I'm jeopardizing her reputation as well, Marion thought, and felt a twinge of guilt. Perhaps it was all wrong . . . She pinched that thought before it grew too uncomfortable. She would leave the Gold Room later, she reasoned, no one the wiser of her identity.

Amelia had given her the tasteful gift of a jewel-encrusted quizzing glass so that she could discard her spectacles for the evening. Still, she wore a tight silk half-mask on her face to better hide her identity. The unusual eyeglass lent an originality to Marion's appearance, and she loved the sensation of elegance it gave her. For one evening she could pretend that she was a lady of the world, a sought-after beauty that the gentlemen fought over.

She played a few hands of cards, and buoyed by a winning streak, she thought she was floating on clouds. In a lull of the game, Marion leveled her quizzing glass at the gentleman just entering the gilded double doors of the Gold Room.

She had waited a long time for Lord Edgewater to reappear into her life. At dawn as she lay sleepless in her bed, she often fantasized about their next meeting and how effortlessly she would win Laurel Manor back from him.

Now there he was, only a few steps away from her on this seductive spring night. A light breeze from the open balcony doors ruffled his hair. His presence sent a jolt of dread mixed with anticipation through her. Marion hoped he would not recognize her in her dashing wig and mask. Yet, she found herself wishing fervently that she was beautiful enough to impress him. Hardly likely, she thought with a sigh. He wouldn't be impressed. Nothing stirred him.

She loathed him and his callous offer of marriage. It pained her to know that he had no more regard for her than a piece of horseflesh at Tattersall's. Actually, he probably had more regard for his horse than he had for her. If only she'd been beautiful, if only he'd been interested in her! If he cared about her, she could carry off this revenge with more panache. She longed to hurt him, just as he'd wounded her.

This evening she wore a rather drab brown chemise gown with gold braiding around the neckline and the hem, and matching slippers. It was one of Aunt Adele's old gowns that had been altered to fit her. A fringed shawl hung from the bend of her elbows, and she spread her chickenskin fan wide to shield her face.

Had she really once traveled with him through the night? An eternity of humiliation had happened since then.

As she stared at him, he lazily lifted his glass and let the glance from one magnified eye rake her over from head to toe. Amelia waved at him, and he sauntered toward their table. Marion's heart fluttered madly, and her hands began to tremble with the tension.

The earl squeezed Amelia's fingers as he bent to place a kiss on her cheek. "What in the world, Amy—" he began—"I didn't expect to find you here. It's most unorthodox—"

Amy slapped his wrist. "Don't berate me, Pierce. It won't happen again, but I couldn't resist the temptation to see how the other side of the world plays. You know I always liked an adventure. Besides, I thought you might come here for a hand of piquet tonight."

"They serve a deuced good supper here, you know. My chef isn't half as good as the expert working here." He turned to Marion, and she could not return his glance without blushing.

He looked singularly attractive in black evening clothes, his face sun-bronzed and his expression amused. He wore a snowy-white cravat folded into a style known as the Waterfall. He looked taller than she remembered, the black evening coat flattering his broad shoulders.

"Miss Milo, my pleasure!" he drawled after Amelia had introduced them. "But surely you must let me escort you home this very minute."

Marion lost her voice as she gazed into the cool gray eyes. He took her outstretched fingers and placed a light kiss on the tips.

"Milo, this is Litton, Lord Edgewater."

"I know . . . well, I've heard of you, and I . . . thought . . . I mean—"

Amelia gave a peal of laughter. "She's quite overcome with you, Pierce. Do be nice to her." She winked at Marion. "Now, Milo, see to it that Litton loses some of his funds tonight."

Marion's concentration was momentarily distracted as

she spied her cousin Melvin by the door. Amelia, who had been introduced to him at a ball, recognized him, too. On a cloud of lavender scent, she left, stopping only to speak with Melvin and beckoning him to follow her. From the corner of her eye Marion noticed that her cousin gave her a long stare across the room.

"I never thought we would meet again this soon, stripling," Litton said dryly. "What has happened to the bonfire? I quite liked it." He studied her wig through the quizzing glass. "This is not the thing—much too tame for you. Why the disguise?"

CHAPTER

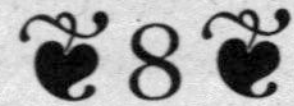

"SO YOU DO RECOGNIZE ME! I SUSPECTED AS MUCH. AREN'T YOU surprised to see me here?" Marion had never felt more foolish in her life. "I thought you might not know me."

His voice was brimming with sarcasm. "Nothing you do surprises me, Miss Marion. In all honesty, I did not recognize you at first, but I've only met one person with that many freckles and such frank eyes. Not even a mask and a generous dusting of rice powder could hide them." He frowned. "This isn't exactly the place for a young, respectable lady. I'm surprised that Amy brought you here. In fact, you must let me escort you home this very minute!"

Marion shook her head. "I know that as a gentleman you feel pressed to protect me, but you cannot force me to leave. Where my friend Amelia goes, I go. It is as simple as that."

He cast a speculative glance at the loud-voiced gentlemen at the faro table. "Amy is a widow. She doesn't have to worry about her reputation quite as much as you." He pinned her with a hard stare. "Seems to me that you don't care one iota about propriety, Miss Rothwell. When you become my wife, I expect you to behave with a bit more circumspection."

"But I'm not your wife, and I have no intention of marrying you, or anyone. Why should I take orders from you? Look for someone else to bully.'' Her voice lowered into an angry whisper. ''Besides, you don't really want me. A marriage to me would be mere convenience for you, nothing more. After the ceremony you would 'bury' me at Laurel Manor and promptly forget about me. I know your sort, always thinking about yourself.''

''By Jove, you're an expert on human nature, aren't you?'' he drawled and leaned back in his chair. He studied the young woman and found her so lovely it created an ache in his heart. It wasn't her appearance—which was more striking than beautiful—but the animation of her personality which shone through and suffused her entire person. Against his better judgment, the earl found himself quite dazzled. She shouldn't be in this sordid gambling salon, but he admired her daring, her breaking of the rules. Ever since he'd met her, flaunting the Society codes was all she'd ever done. He felt an urge to laugh out loud, but she wouldn't like that. He would stick closely to her side to protect her from any rude, inebriated lout, and as soon as the opportunity presented itself, he would bundle her off home.

''I take it Laurel Manor means more to you than anything else in the world,'' he asked, his voice more teasing than he'd wished. ''It has added a headache to my usually smooth estate affairs.''

Marion fanned her heated face, growing angrier as he grew calmer. ''A tall, strong gentleman like you ought to be able to handle the responsibility of one well-kept estate like Laurel Manor.''

His eyes darkened one shade, and she hoped it was from wrath. She longed to make him angry, as furious as she was. However, his tone of voice remained steady as he spoke. ''I believe you're the most impolite and cynical lady I've ever had the misfortune to encounter.'' His gaze traveled lazily the length of her body. ''If a very shapely one.''

"Milord! Flattery won't bring about my surrender. By turning down your marriage proposal I hope I shook you out of your loathsome complacency." She took a deep breath. "You needed that. The world doesn't revolve around you, after all."

He chuckled, but his eyes had narrowed with anger and his smile was forced. "I can't say that I feel particularly shaken."

"If it weren't for you, I would be rid of the Winthrops and I would have a glorious time in Burnham—a tenfold better fate than my current one."

She glanced at the earl to see what impact her words were having. For an enemy, he made her curiously weak-kneed. She wished she could beat him at piquet this very evening to be done with this farce, but she was still a novice at the game. Amelia maintained she was making great progress but that she had to practice her memory.

"You could be back in Burnham just as soon as I procure a special license and find a clergyman to marry us."

"I still don't understand why you're so eager to wed me. You said yourself you've ducked the marital noose these many years."

"Hmmm, this might be strange logic, but I would feel safe marrying someone who doesn't want me and my wealth. I've never met a lady who would voluntarily turn down such an offer, and that makes me elated. At least I can be sure you wouldn't be marrying me for my title and my estates. What do you say? Not such a bad idea, eh?"

"You seem to think that holy wedlock is no more important than buying a new carriage or a horse. You can't buy me, Lord Edgewater." She changed the subject. "How are things at Laurel Manor? I daresay you never visit the place." A wave of bitterness swelled inside her. How could she maintain a conversation with a man who so callously had taken her inheritance? Amelia had insisted that she pretend not to harbor any grudge toward Pierce Litton, only beat him at his own game.

One magnified eye stared at her, measuring up, speculating.

"I offered to hand it back to you. I'm not in the habit of robbing damsels of their dowry."

"I don't need your pity. My father behaved stupidly, and I cringe to remember that he gambled away the entire estate." She fanned herself vigorously, "And you're ruthless, wholly devoid of any deeper feelings."

He laughed. "And a fool for accepting a tongue-whipping from a stripling."

Marion bristled. "Milord, if I were a man—"

"You would call me out?" A faint smile curled his lips. "Fortunately you aren't, or I would surely come to my end prematurely." A wicked light flared in his eyes. "I'm glad I found you again. My life has been unbearably dull since I last saw you."

Marion could not stop her heart from quivering with pleasure. No one had ever presented her such a handsome compliment. "I daresay you're laughing behind my back," she muttered. She watched him pull out a snuffbox, extract a few grains, and with an elegant twist of his wrist inhale the snuff.

His lips twitched. "I have better things to do."

Marion glanced furtively across the room at Melvin standing by the faro bank. His face shone red with excitement, and perspiration wet the chestnut strands brushed across his forehead. "Looks like Cousin Melvin has inherited my father's reckless streak—and misfortune." She tapped her folded fan thoughtfully against her fingertips. "Where does he get the funds? Uncle Bertram is singularly close-fisted. He always tries to borrow money from me, the rat!''

''I daresay his luck is not always rotten. In fact, I saw him win five hundred pounds at Brook's last night.''

Marion gasped. ''Five hundred pounds! You must be bamming me.''

''No, it's the truth. Since I'm here, I suppose I ought to lose some of my money, to keep this ship floating,'' the earl said with a sigh and looked toward the faro table.

Marion could not resist the temptation to challenge the earl. ''Would you care to play a hand of piquet with me?''

Again his eyes raked over her. ''You?'' He seemed to ponder the offer. ''I suppose you are not as innocent as you look after all, but I would hate to fleece a stripling.''

Marion straightened her small, slim body and stared him belligerently in the eye. ''You're very rude, milord. Soon you'll regret that you ever said those words.''

''A master at the game, are you?'' He swung his eyeglass carelessly on its ribbon.

''Not precisely, but Amelia says I have aptitude. I daresay I inherited that from Father.'' She eagerly waited for his response. ''Well?''

''No.''

Her anger increased at his dismissal. She bit back an angry retort, remembering that Amelia had warned her to keep her temper at bay. Amelia had stressed the importance of learning the weaknesses of the opposite sex and acting from that knowledge with tact and finesse. What man could resist a soft and graceful female? She still felt far from possessing such attributes . . . However, Marion secretly desired to become assured and graceful to impress the earl. Not that she wanted to admit that fact, not even to herself. Yet, she burned to acquire the same elegance of bearing as Amelia.

"If I may tear you from your pleasant dreams, stripling, I'd like your company at the supper table. The dining room looks empty. Amy can join us if she likes. All this bickering has made me quite famished."

Marion's gaze flew to his face, and she saw the devilish twinkle in his eyes. "Your intolerable bluntness grates on my nerves, milord," she said heatedly. "If I were a more delicate female, you would take pains to treat me with all due respect."

"I would ask no simpering miss to join me for supper," he retorted. "I like your fire."

Her ire dwindled into nothing. "Oh." Round-eyed, she placed her gloved hand upon his arm. Stealing a glance at Amelia, she saw her mentor wink with encouragement. "Yes, thank you, milord, I accept."

Over a light repast of cold salmon, white crusty bread, and champagne, Pierce Litton scrutinized his spirited companion. The wig she wore failed to flatter her thin pixie face, and he was unaccountably annoyed with Amelia for taking Miss Marion under her wing. Why had she done that?

In all his days on the town, he had never met a young woman as refreshing and innocent as Marion Rothwell, and he hated to see the frankness, the sweetness, wilt from her eyes to be replaced with cunning and coquetry, which would invariably happen as worldliness took the place of innocence. It was sure to happen at a place like this.

He didn't doubt that Marion had badgered Amelia into taking her to the Gold Room, but why? Marion was planning something; he was sure of that. He would soon discover the truth.

Marion had been right; he'd planned to marry her to escape the tireless match-making mamas and to relinquish his interest in Laurel Manor. But now he found that the prospect of marriage intrigued him. Perhaps he'd gone about proposing in the wrong way. He'd never dreamed that she would reject him. She had—and in no uncertain terms! It titillated him like nothing else. Mayhap it was time that he got married and set up his nursery. If nothing else, Mother would be elated. It was unlikely that he would fall in love with the young woman. He'd never been in love, and at twenty-seven it was probably too late. Marion would not fall in love with him; she was too angry for that. But if he played his cards right, he might get her to surrender and accept his offer. Marriage to her might be quite amusing . . .

Marion spent a pleasant hour in the earl's company, laughing at his dry wit. She was hopelessly taken in by his charm. For charming he could be when he wanted to; he had shown her that the first time they met.

A haze of champagne fumes rose to her head and she laughed helplessly. As he stretched out his long legs, she studied his calves. "I'm sure your silk stockings do not need a filling of sawdust, like those of Sir Cedric 'Clodpole,' to make your calves look rounder."

Litton's lips quirked upward. "Singularly perceptive of you to notice that." He thoughtfully chewed a piece of salmon as he studied her face.

She wondered if she had a smudge on her nose.

"I do hope you're not in the habit of giving compliments to all the adoring blades around you, Marion. I warn you, it'll make me quite jealous."

Marion remembered her uncle's conversation with Sir Cedric and shuddered with revulsion. "If you're thinking of Sir Cedric, you may rest assured that I've said no such thing to him. He needs all the padding his tailor can conceive." She almost choked on her last words, and her eyes filled with panic as she noticed the man in the dining room doorway, Sir Cedric himself, followed by her cousin Melvin.

The two young gentlemen nodded to Edgewater and stared at Marion.

"Good evening, Edgewater," Melvin said.

If they recognized her, Uncle Bertram would hear of this evening, Marion thought and fell into a paroxysm of coughing, hiding her face behind the linen napkin. As the earl solicitously offered to pound her on the back, she impatiently refused his assistance.

"I say, your lady friend must have a dreadful cold," Melvin commented. When the earl didn't reply, he continued, "You've met Sir Cedric Longpole, of course." The two men bowed stiffly, and the earl had to admit that, as Marion had said at their first meeting, the fellow had the face of a frog. At this moment the cheeks were very red, as if Sir Cedric had imbibed too much drink.

"Servant," Lord Edgewater murmured and rose, shielding the coughing Marion from their view. He leveled his quizzing glass at the young men.

"I admire your neckcloth, Edgewater," said Sir Cedric. "Perhaps you can teach me to fold the Mathematical some time. I'm very partial to that style."

"Good God!" said the earl. "Who is your valet?"

"I'm afraid he doesn't have a flair for neckcloths, and neither do I," Sir Cedric said in his high-pitched voice.

"Practice, is all it is," the earl replied, bored.

Marion suffered another paroxysm of mirth and kicked him under the table. He smiled appreciatively, and her eyes teared with withheld laughter.

"My man is much annoyed with me as I crumple twenty neckcloths every morning," Sir Cedric continued. "I firmly believe there must be some secret to it."

"I assure you, there is no secret behind it. Furthermore, I do not think the matter of neckcloths is a suitable subject to discuss in the presence of a lady. And now, if you excuse us, I have to take Miss Brown outside for some air before she suffocates.'' He bowed stiffly and helped Marion, who was still hiding behind her napkin, to rise. Leaning heavily on the earl's arm, she escaped from the two gaping men.

On the terrace at the back of the house, she said, still laughing, ''Didn't I tell you? Any fate is better than marrying Sir Cedric, the Clodpole.'' She remembered Sir Cedric's pact with her uncle, and her mirth died.

''I quite agree with you, but one almost feels a trifle sorry for the fellow. Life cannot be easy for him—with a face like that.''

Marion smiled. At least the earl had a sense of humor, even if everything else about him was ''wrong.'' Or was it? Had she overlooked his personality in her anger? She breathed deeply of the cool night air, perfumed with the scent of woodbine that grew on a trellis along the wall.

''Thank you for saving me, Lord Edgewater. Sir Cedric might have recognized me, wig or no wig. And you were lucky to get away from him. There is no stopping him when he starts his chatter. Nothing but inanities fall from his lips.'' She frowned with puzzlement. ''I don't understand why Papa at all supported Uncle Bertram's suggestion that I marry Sir Cedric.'' She chewed on her bottom lip. ''How could a loving parent wish such an ill fate on his only daughter?''

''He would like to see you safely settled, no doubt. You said Sir Cedric was your only suitor . . . until you met me.''

Marion stood quiet and pensive. Her life seemed to consist of jumping from one tussock to another in an endless quagmire of confusion. ''I wish Papa had spoken to me of his difficulties instead of sending me off to London.''

''What did you say, stripling?'' Lord Edgewater's voice

sounded very close to her ear, low and husky, tickling her. She gasped with surprise. What was he doing?

"Afraid of me?" he murmured, his voice relaxed and teasing once more.

"Oh . . . no, not at all." The champagne she'd drunk earlier had eased away her insecurities for the moment, and she could almost believe that she was beautiful. She peered at him in the darkness. "You know, this is like that night you almost killed me on Grafton Street, so dark I can only see your teeth."

His hands cupped her shoulders, palms warm through the thin material of her gown. "You smell enchantingly, and the night is oddly . . . dangerous. Don't you agree? It must be the potent air of spring." He gently pulled her back against him, still gripping her shoulders.

"You think so?" Marion held her breath in wonder. She felt his hard body press against her, and a rush of delicious anticipation shot through her. She had no idea that the closeness of a man could create such sensations in her body. An exquisite rivulet of delight spiraled through her as she felt the soft butterfly kiss of his warm lips at the nape of her neck.

"What are you doing?" she croaked, her voice lost in this new wonder.

He muttered something unintelligible and slowly released her. He cleared his throat. "Madness, pure madness."

Marion stared at him, her eyes unfocused. He bowed. "I beg your pardon for taking such liberties, but as I implied, this lovely night air sends madness through my veins."

Marion wasn't sure what she felt. Mostly she regretted that the strange, wondrous moment had passed. She peered at the brilliant stars through her quizzing glass. "You're right, the night is singularly beautiful." She felt her insecurity return. She knew he had overstepped the boundaries of gentlemanly behavior, but she quite liked it. Would she dare to tell him that?

"I suppose you behaved like a—a rake? But I think I enjoyed it." She turned to him eagerly. "Have you kissed many ladies?"

His teeth gleamed white and a low chuckle rumbled in his chest. "I don't keep count."

In a small voice, she added, "I've never been kissed. Do you think you could . . . show me how? I guess you're as good a teacher as any. And I know you wouldn't go gossiping about it."

"It's not the thing, stripling. It would be like robbing the cradle."

"Not at all! I'm eighteen, an age when one is very eligible for marriage." Chagrined, she turned her back on him, only to hear him take a step closer. "You think I'm silly."

"Your body is far advanced for your age, well shaped and seductive in all the right places. However, your innocence is so very precious, and I hate to be the one to put that 'knowing' look into your eyes."

"Fustian!" Enthusiastically she tilted her face toward him. Her senses swam when his hands closed over her shoulders, and as he pulled her into his embrace intimately, her breasts pressed against his hard chest. The novel sensation made her quite breathless. She could sense his rapid heartbeat. His lips, warm and smiling, touched hers, lightly at first, and as she did not shy away, more determinedly.

She wanted to swoon at this new rapture. Lifted onto a cloud, she was only aware of his lips moving against hers, his tongue touching her teeth, teasing the soft inside of her lips, robbing her of her breath, of equilibrium, of herself; consuming her, burning, caressing.

For a long time she stood pressed to his chest, his jaw resting lightly on top of her head, her nostrils filled with his alluring male scent, her cheek feeling the thudding of his heart. *Heaven.*

"I think I liked that very much," she whispered. "You obviously have a lot of knowledge in this area."

"I wouldn't want to brag," he said, frowning at his own reaction to the kiss. If Miss Marion was dazed by the powerful experience, he was amazed at the sweetness that had filled him as soon as his lips touched hers. It must be the peculiar seductive air of the night. An odd reluctance to release her haunted him, as if it meant tearing a priceless cord that had been created between them.

CHAPTER

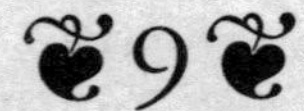

MARION FELT AS IF SHE'D GROWN WINGS AS SHE RETURNED TO THE gambling salon on Lord Edgewater's arm. Her head spun in delicious abandon. No champagne could have brought such rapture as the earl's kiss had given her.

She ventured a glance at him and noticed that he looked somewhat bemused. Had the kiss touched him as deeply as it had her, she wondered? For a moment her delight dimmed as she remembered that she oughtn't to have sneaked into the seductive spring night and kissed her enemy. But just for a moment she would pretend that they weren't adversaries.

Along one wall a series of curtained alcoves were set up for suppers *à deux,* and Marion noted couples dining and chatting in the dim light. For one wild instant she almost pulled the earl into one of the empty rooms to explore further what surprises lovemaking might bring. She quelled her impulse at the last moment. It wouldn't do to continue this dangerous if heady trail.

As they reached the doors leading to the brighter light of the main salon, they encountered Melvin and Sir Cedric. In the last moment, Marion drew back in the shadow of the gold velvet drapery festooning the opening.

"Ah! There you are," Sir Cedric exclaimed to the earl.

''I was looking for you.'' He threw a cursory glance at Marion, showing no interest in her.

Melvin, however, gave her a long stare, and she fluttered her fan in front of her face. She heaved a sigh of relief as he looked away without recognizing her.

''What did you want to see me about?'' The earl sounded mildly surprised.

''Sir Cedric is getting leg-shackled,'' Melvin blurted out, and Sir Cedric nudged him in the ribs.

The earl smiled sardonically. ''Am I invited to the wedding?''

Sir Cedric shifted his weight from one foot to the other. ''Actually, I only wanted to ask you a small favor. Would you find it agreeable to lend me your valet for that day? To tie my neckcloth, y'know.''

The earl laughed. ''Well! That's a favor I can't refuse. The bridegroom must go to the altar looking his best.''

Sir Cedric wrung his hands in delight. ''Thank you! I'm indebted to you.''

The earl slanted a curious glance at Marion, then returned his attention to Sir Cedric. ''Who's the lovely bride?''

''Oh, the announcement hasn't been posted in the papers, but it's only a matter of days. The arrangement is settled with her guardian. I'm marrying Miss Marion Rothwell—not the most beautiful of marital 'prizes,' but then neither am I.''

Marion flinched as if he'd slapped her, and the earl's shoulders stiffened. Marion was aware of a slow anger rising in him. ''Hmm, with her guardian? Has the young lady accepted you?'' he asked.

Sir Cedric scratched his head. ''Eh . . . well, every time I've tried to approach her lately, she's been unavailable.''

Liar! Marion thought, infuriated.

''Lord Winthrop has promised me she'll be home tomorrow morning. I shall speak with her then, but I believe she has no say in the matter—not after her uncle makes her see reason.''

Marion's anger grew until she could barely contain herself. She whipped her fan harder to keep her temper under control.

''She's a meek young lady, then?'' the earl asked in his infuriating drawl.

''Hardly!'' Melvin spat. ''Marion is a wild one, and no mistake. Does exactly as she pleases without any thought to others.''

Marion could now have clouted the three men, and as the earl winked at her, she could barely suppress her ire.

''By the way,'' Melvin continued, ''I've heard that you're planning to sell off part of the land that was her inheritance.''

Marion's ears burned and her mind reeled at this startling piece of news. The earl slanted another cautious glance at her.

''How did you hear that rumor?'' he asked Melvin.

''I'm related to the chit, remember. My father heard through the estate agents—''

''Sir Bertram shouldn't listen too closely to mere hearsay. However, I can't oversee too many estates. It would take all my time.''

Sir Cedric drew up his sloping shoulders. ''If it weren't for you, my lord, I would soon be the owner of those lands. I quite resent your—''

Marion took a step forward, but the earl barred her with one arm. ''I think Miss Brown is getting bored with our conversation. Perhaps we can continue at another time.''

The two young men glanced at Marion, and she stepped back at the last moment. If Melvin recognized her, she would lose her only chance at winning back the estate. If her uncle found out that she'd visited the gambling salon, he would marry her off to Sir Cedric faster than she could blink.

"I—I feel faint," she whispered, and hurried back toward the terrace doors. The night closed behind her, and she clung to the marble balustrade for support. At this moment, she could kill the earl—as well as the others who'd dismissed her for something less than a doormat. Wait until she had a chance to avenge herself for their cruelty! Not that their slander was news, but the truth of her plight hurt the same every time.

As she gulped for air, she was vaguely aware of footsteps behind her.

"You didn't have to run away," the earl said, much too casually, Marion thought.

"Why should I remain and listen to more painful barbs? I regret that I didn't leave earlier. Then you could have discussed me at closer detail with the 'lads.'" She whirled and faced him, fists knotted. "I detest you! Of all the men in the world, you're the most unreliable, cunning . . ." She lost her breath as she sought for another, more scalding epithet.

"I had no idea that the rumors would spread so quickly. I merely mentioned the idea to your father."

"How dare you be so cool about it! My father worked all his life improving the land of Laurel Manor—for me. I can't believe you would consider dividing the estate. It's one of the most prosperous holdings in the area."

"Just for that reason. I could invest elsewhere, since I have no interest in Somerset. My other estates are in Essex and Leicestershire—in the opposite direction to Somerset, so to say. I was only trying to be practical—"

"Heartless! That's what you are. You don't care for anyone but yourself and your own comforts." She pushed him in the chest so hard that he stumbled backward. "You even went so far as to make an effort to trick me into marriage. Then you would have sold the estate only to spite me."

"S'faith, that's preposterous!"

He moved toward her, but she shoved him again. "Get out of my way! If Papa suffers another apoplexy, I shall hold you responsible." She stormed back into the salon. When she found Amelia, she complained about a sudden headache and asked to return home.

When she got back to the privacy of her bedchamber on Albemarle Street, she would retire and not get up until she had a plan for revenge. She would find a fitting punishment, not only for the earl, but for Sir Cedric, who thought he could marry her without as much as a by-your-leave. They might have found her naive, but she was no fool. That they would soon discover . . .

CHAPTER 10

Pierce Litton, the Earl of Edgewater, spent a sleepless night on a sofa in his book-lined study at the Edgewater mansion in Hanover Square. No pink-and-gold rays of dawn prodded him out of a bed, as he'd neglected to seek the privacy of his bedchamber on the previous evening. All because of a certain impudent miss. *Marion Rothwell.* The name echoed in his mind for the thousandth time, and he wished he could dislodge the disturbing memories of her in that unbecoming brassy wig! That kiss had shaken his world, and it was no use thinking that it hadn't. It was her innocence that touched him every time he saw her, and that agile mind of hers. He never knew what she would say next, and it intrigued him like nothing else.

Standing by the tall windows, he watched the city come to life. Although not many people moved on Hanover Square at this early hour of the morning, the air filled with the raucous voices of the hawkers with their wooden carts offering fresh fish, milk, and barrels of ale. He heard the servants stir in the kitchen region, and a faint smell of smoke reached his nose. Someone was starting a fire in the hearth, a fire that would cook his breakfast in due time. He had never cooked anyone's breakfast, let alone his own . . . The very thought of doing it had never occurred to him.

Was he really so cruel and thoughtless as Miss Marion had suggested? The question nagged at him incessantly. Had he grown so arrogant over the years that he no longer had any consideration for others? Strangely shaken, he paced the room. In passing, he gave the gleaming pianoforte a loving stroke and debated whether to start playing. But no, he would awaken the whole house. Anyway, according to his father, playing the pianoforte was not the accepted pastime of a gentleman . . . It had been so long since he last enjoyed a morning of soothing music. A poignant memory struck him. One night—he must have been eighteen—when he finished composing his first sonata in the music room at Litton Place, it had all come to an end. He'd never felt so alive, so fulfilled. Euphoria had bubbled in his veins. He hadn't noticed his father standing in the darkened doorway, but he recalled every nuance of the pain as his parent had slammed the lid of the pianoforte down over his fingers. The joints of his knuckles seemed still to ache at the memory.

"Pierce, I don't want to ever find you in here with your shirt sleeves rolled up and your neckcloth all askew. What kind of behavior is that? Not that of a gentleman, surely. From now on, you'll show some spine!"

Father's eyes had been so cold and disapproving, his voice icy. The earl recoiled as he recalled that he'd almost cried. His hands had ached abominably for days. After that incident, Father had kept him busy traveling among their holdings on business—when he wasn't at the university. Father had always taken every opportunity to imprint his derogatory views of music.

What had become of those old compositions? Had his parent destroyed them? He cringed with an inexplicable worry, as if life had suddenly become intolerable. These painful memories that had been buried so deep now stirred—all because of a tender kiss. What madness had possessed him on the previous night? He hadn't planned to kiss the chit with the wild red hair, yet he'd been compelled to do it.

An unlucky star must have shone on him when he had chanced upon Marion that very first night in Grafton Street. The last thing he needed this morning, or any other morning, was to be reminded of a pair of green innocent eyes and soft lips, but he seemed unable to dismiss the memory. To distract his thoughts he went down to breakfast. He knew he was in for a bout of insomnia again, and the thought lowered his spirit.

His mother, the Dowager Countess of Edgewater, was already at the breakfast table as he stepped into the dining room. He gave her an unintentional scowl, and her eyebrows rose a notch in question.

"If your sour face is any proof, you must have had a bad run of luck at the tables last night," she said with a smile. She was a large, elegant woman of a humorous, independent disposition, traits that kept mother and son in good charity with each other. Every year, the dowager stayed at Hanover Square during the Season. She always shared breakfast with the earl, although she led her own busy life in town, a life that seldom crossed paths with that of the earl.

"Yes, a deuced bad run of luck." He angrily flipped the pages of *The Gazette*.

"You're behaving just like your father, you know." The dowager bit into a piece of buttered toast. "When something stirred him, he used to be angry for days. Care to speak about it?"

"No, I've been an utter fool, that's all. And I've been

listening to gossip—rumors about my business dealings in Somerset. There's a limit to a man's patience."

"I daresay. You never had an abundance of patience." The dowager sipped her hot tea gingerly and sent her son a shrewd glance. "How much did you lose?"

"Ahem . . ." He didn't want to tell an outright lie, so he gave his parent an evasive answer. "More than enough. I shan't attend the Gold Room again. The play is much too deep there."

The dowager laughed. "Didn't stop you before."

He didn't deign to answer that. Could he tell her about his encounter with the infuriating Miss Rothwell? Still scowling, he bent over a plate of kippers and eggs. Companionable silence filled the room as they busied themselves with the meal. Griggs, the butler, carried in a plate with grilled ham that emitted an appetizing aroma. He refilled their cups and left.

"Say, Mother, what do you know of the Rothwells of Burnham, Somerset."

"Concerning the estate you acquired so suddenly? Yes, it's an old respectable family. Has no big scandals that I know of, except for the loss of Laurel Manor to you." She drank some tea and continued.

"I believe the only child, a daughter, is one of this year's debutantes. She's sponsored by the Winthrop dullards. They are not well liked in this town. If my memory doesn't fail me, Sir Bertram is pompous and quite coldhearted, and Lady Winthrop has a weak constitution, or she pretends to have one. It doesn't surprise me that Marion hasn't been a success, since they give her no encouragement, no support. A young woman needs someone to teach her all the niceties, and the poor soul lost her mother very early. She has no polish. I've heard the Winthrops have accepted an offer from that dreadful man, Sir Cedric Longpole."

The earl laughed. "He wants to borrow my valet for the occasion, to tie his neckcloth."

"Of all the—! I wonder if they'll outfit Miss Rothwell in style. I've heard that her ballgowns are made from Lady Winthrop's castoffs. That's especially bad *ton,* and I pity Miss Rothwell." She gave him a speculative glance. "You do remember her, don't you? The young lady had hair like . . . like a—"

"Bonfire," Litton supplied gloomily.

"Yes. Very unusual. Lady Winthrop should have summoned a hairdresser. A pity she needs to wear spectacles."

"Blind as a bat." Litton took a deep draught of ale.

"You seem to know a lot about her. How odd, to be sure! I thought you held all debutantes in contempt."

"I do, dammit! Simpering misses, all of them, in a pink-and-white way."

The dowager stopped eating, halting her fork in midair. "My word! How very strange an expression, Pierce."

"I'm only echoing someone else's opinion." *Marion's.* He threw the paper to the table with an irate twist of his hand. "What do you think of Miss Rothwell?"

A smile spread across the dowager's dignified face. She shook her head. "Pierce, I say! Miss Rothwell must have chipped a piece out of your granite heart. I have never heard you talk like this before." She thought for a moment, then patted his hand. "I'll see what else I can find out about her."

"Don't bother. I'm not interested in continuing my acquaintance with her."

"I had no idea that you already knew her."

His eyes bored into the dowager's identical gray ones. "Promise that you won't breathe a word of this to anyone. I'll wring your lovely neck if you do."

''Can't risk that,'' the dowager said with a chiding smile. ''Mum it is, Pierce.''

Litton told her everything from the first moment he had set eyes on Marion, only leaving out the kiss.

''Goodness gracious! Miss Marion in the Gold Room, among rakes and libertines?'' The dowager stared with outrage at her son. ''Her reputation'll be utterly destroyed. You should have taken her home.''

''I tried, but she refused. She was with Amelia Milford, who is utterly trustworthy. But if Amy continues to frequent the gambling hells with Miss Marion, sooner or later the chit's true identity is bound to come out. Then, indeed, her reputation will be in shreds. I have wracked my brain to find a way to make her accept Laurel Manor as a gift, but not even an earthquake could shake sense into her. She declined the offer. She literally bristled with pride.''

''What a strange creature!'' The dowager's eyes twinkled. ''Set you on your head, did she?''

''She has a way with her,'' he grumbled. ''I feel an inexplicable responsibility for the brat. Most vexing.'' He stared at the pale green-and-blue carpet and the polished cherry wood table, but those objects could give him no answers. ''At the Gold Room she was as misplaced as a lily in the desert.''

''Exposed to rakes and reprobates like yourself, eh?'' The dowager gave an exaggerated sigh. ''Your reputation of a gambler is greatly blown out of proportion after the infamous gamble of Laurel Manor, but I suppose you don't mind that. Anything to keep the matchmakers at bay, eh? The debutantes tremble in their satin slippers with fear as you walk by.''

''Mother, if you continue in this vein I shall order you out of my presence. You'll be forced to wither away at your little gloomy dower house in Essex or at Litton Place in

Leicestershire,'' he threatened, but a faint smile lurked in his eyes.

''I will return to Leicestershire only when the Season is over,'' the dowager said with finality. ''And I have a mind to pay Miss Rothwell a visit one of these mornings. One can't trust the judgment of a gentleman. Perhaps I'll meet her at the gambling salon. I don't mind losing a few guineas at the tables. Are females allowed into the sanctum of the Gold Room?''

''*Ladies* do not attend.''

The dowager smiled a cunning smile. The earl knew that in her heyday she had not been averse to a hand of silver loo or piquet in some ''forbidden'' gaming salon.

''Well then, I suppose I will have to make a formal visit to still my curiosity about the Rothwell miss. Any female who has the power to make a dent in your hardened heart is worth some scrutiny.''

The earl gave her an entreating glance. ''Mother, I'm not that cynical, am I?''

She patted his hand. ''You are, y'know. It's because you haven't found love—yet. But you will.''

''Mother! You're an incorrigible romantic. Don't expect me to escort you to Albemarle Street. I'll stay as far away as possible from the Winthrops, which won't be difficult.'' He waved a letter in front of her eyes. ''This calls me to Leicestershire. Business as usual.''

''Oh. When can I expect you back here?''

''It might take a few days.'' He frowned. ''I desperately need some pure country air to clear the fog of idiocy from my brain, and get some sleep.''

''Scheming mothers will tear their hair out in despair, and daughters will wither away in frustrated longing, especially Emily Ralston.''

The earl groaned with disgust. ''Mother! If you know

what is good for you, don't remind me of Miss Ralston's determined efforts to snare me—''

Tinkling laughter was the only answer he received as his parent left the room.

That morning Marion, heavy-eyed, forced herself out of bed to attend breakfast with the Winthrops and pretend she had slept innocently all night in her bed when in fact she'd been planning her revenge on the two men she loathed most, Sir Cedric and the Earl of Edgewater.

''I don't understand how you can look so wan this morning after retiring at nine o'clock last night,'' Aunt Adele said to Marion while attacking her dry toast with the butter knife. Her eyes bored into Marion, who still struggled with the ghost of sleep that threatened to engulf her. Little did Aunt Adele know that she'd sneaked to the Gold Room when the house was quiet.

''You know you have a lot to do today, Marion, first helping Mrs. Fawley mend the linens, then continue cataloging the books. Then Sir Cedric will come and see you, and this time you shall give him the answer that he's seeking.''

''Or else?'' Marion fought the twinge of fear in her heart.

Aunt Adele gave her a strange look. ''Really, Marion! He has the right to see you since your nuptials aren't far off. He wants to set the date, and you will make sure to comply with any suggestion he might have. You're very fortunate to have received such an advantageous offer; you should be suitably grateful.''

Derisive laughter cackled on the second floor from Prinny, who was the most active in the morning.

''I cannot abide that bird!'' Sir Bertram discarded the morning paper and glared down his nose. ''I wish I could have some peace at breakfast for once. All this chattering is fatal to my digestion.''

Marion might not have disliked her uncle so much if it weren't for the deal with Sir Cedric that she'd overheard. He pinned her with a chastising glare. ''I heard all about your little games to avoid Sir Cedric. Today is your last chance to accept him gracefully. Marriage to him is the perfect solution to your problems.''

When Marion opened her mouth to protest, he waved his hand irritably. ''You're marrying him, and that's the end of it! You have tried my patience long enough as it is.''

''Hear, hear,'' echoed Melvin with a nasty smile.

Marion kicked him under the table, and he pinched his lips into an angry line. His eyes promised retribution, but Marion wasn't afraid of him.

''I don't see any evidence that Sir Cedric harbors tender feelings toward me,'' she said to the room at large.

A chill ran through Marion as Sir Bertram's cold eyes turned to her again. She'd thought of tactics to put off the wedding, but she was trapped. Now that Sir Bertram had returned, she knew it was fruitless to argue. Still, a last try wouldn't hurt. ''I fail to understand his interest now that I've lost my inheritance.'' She picked at her food, wondering what lies would come next.

Her relatives' uneasy glances did not escape her.

''You must know that he cares nothing for your loss of funds,'' Aunt Adele said and patted her hand.

Marion expelled a weary sigh. ''That's a plumper if I ever heard one. Sir Cedric cares naught for me. If he did, he wouldn't pester me with unwelcome advances.''

''Pester you?'' Aunt Adele's eyes grew rounder. ''Then a speedy wedding is essential.''

Marion knotted her hands into fists under the tablecloth.

"Sir Cedric would be unable to find a lady willing to marry him with that toadlike face and oily manners of his."

"Dashed impudence! I'm appalled at your rudeness. Do not speak about your future bridegroom in such terms! No, I'm quite out of tolerance with you, Marion." Uncle Bertram's face took on a bull-like aspect, chin pressed down toward chest, eyes piercing under a scowling bar of eyebrows. Marion shivered with unease.

Melvin, who usually slept till noon, piped, "Yes, Cedric is growing more impatient every day." He sniggered, and Marion sent another well-aimed blow at his leg. This time he was expecting it, and her toes connected with the chair leg. Suppressing a howl of pain, she glared at her cousin. With an angelic smile, he shrugged his shoulders.

She had no time to lose. She had to win Laurel Manor back before they forced her bodily to the altar with Sir Cedric. She would beg her father to intervene, even though he'd appointed Uncle Bertram her guardian. Even if his mind wandered, Papa would have to be made to understand her point of view.

Standing on unsteady legs, she said, "Uncle, may I leave the table? I have to plan for my meeting with Sir Cedric. To look my best for him, I'll have to change my dress."

Sir Bertram nodded, and she laid down her napkin and fled out of the room. Melvin's giggles followed her up the stairs.

Pacing the floor, she agonized over ways to make the slippery Sir Cedric pay for pretending to love her. It hurt even more than Melvin's innuendoes that she was as ugly as last week's dinner. She not only was disappointed in Sir Cedric and her family, but also in the Earl of Edgewater. She had begun to like him, and their kiss last night had been a vehicle to ecstasy. Then she'd found out that he had—all along—planned to sell off Laurel Manor land. There was a limit to how much she could take! She wished she could find a way to hurt both men at once, but it might prove to be tricky. Anyway, she knew she wouldn't fall for the earl's smooth seduction ever again! One mistake was enough . . .

She sat down to write a letter to her father and plead with him. If he were lucid, he would verify the earl's intention to sell the land. Oh, God, please let it be only a rumor . . .

CHAPTER 11

Marion had to accept Sir Cedric's offer of marriage to gain some time. Otherwise Uncle Bertram might force a wedding by special license. Not that she had any intention of going through with the ceremony! She felt a pinch of guilt as gifts started to arrive, but they could always be sent back. No, she would never marry Sir Cedric, even if he'd given her an heirloom emerald engagement ring.

Three days later, Amelia sent an invitation to a musical afternoon at her house. The Winthrops were invited, and Marion pointed out to Aunt Adele that she'd rather attend a musicale than a ball. Then she wouldn't have to face the humiliation of being a wallflower.

"Since you're soon to be wed to Sir Cedric, I should hope that problem will no longer be an issue," Lady Winthrop pointed out, then reluctantly agreed to chaperone Marion to Amelia's house. "But I'm not sure about the music. I never liked those string orchestras." She made a delicate shudder. "And as for opera singers, I wouldn't miss them if I never heard another one." She gave Marion a long stare. "It looks to me as if Amelia Milford has taken a liking to you. I gather she's eager to cultivate connections to Society."

"Oh, no, Aunt Adele. She seems to know everybody. I find her entertaining and kind. She's been a good friend when I couldn't find anyone else." *To help me,* she added silently. "It's in the early evening. The musicale won't wear you out like balls do."

Aunt Adele sniffed. "I still think she's an opportunist. Why, we have the entrance to the loftiest of soirées in London."

"So does she, Aunt Adele. Why, she has vouchers to Almack's."

Aunt Adele's eyes popped. "*Almack's?* But only the very highest echelons—"

"Precisely." Marion indulged in a sweet smile.

Aunt Adele opened and closed her mouth like a beached fish. In a huff, she drew her shawls closer around her.

"If I ask very nicely, she might introduce you to Lady Jersey. I know it has always been your dream—"

"Say no more, Marion. This conversation has brought on my palpitations." She fanned herself with the corner of her shawl.

"We will attend, won't we, Aunt Adele?"

"Oh, very well! You're so persistent you give me a headache. By the way, where did you meet this Mrs. Milford?"

"At some ball . . . I don't remember," Marion said vaguely. She didn't want to lie, but if Aunt Adele found out that she'd met Amy on the Bath stagecoach, she would truly have a fit. In a note to Marion, Amelia had mentioned that the earl would attend and that she hoped Marion would get a chance to play a hand of piquet with him. She wished that Marion could win back her estate without having to visit disreputable gambling salons. She had intimated that any more such visits were unthinkable. "Pierce gave me a rakedown after the night at the Gold Room," she wrote. "He called me irresponsible and reckless, and I fear he was right. So, Marion, you must come to my musicale! I've hired an excellent string orchestra, and I've secured a promise from Madame Naldi to sing for us . . ."

Marion put away the note, which had arrived with the invitation. "I look forward to hearing La Naldi," she said.

"Hmph! I didn't know you were so interested in music, only books," Lady Winthrop said and inspected the last rose that Marion had embroidered on the firescreen. "Marion, these stitches are a disgrace!"

Marion snatched the embroidery from her hands. "I have varied interests," she said meekly as her aunt gave her an affronted stare. "Among them music." *And cards,* she added silently.

Amelia sent over a gown of striped blue silk with a lace-trimmed flounce for Marion. In a note, she stated the dress no longer fit her and that she hoped Marion could benefit from her own loss.

Marion was delighted, and with her silver-fringed shawl over her shoulders thought she cut quite a dash as she entered the drawing room at Amelia's house. Spindly gilt chairs had been arranged in rows in front of the dais where the orchestra had set up their instruments. The program promised music by Mr. Handel—part of the Water Music that had been played for the first time in 1717 as George I and a royal party sailed down the Thames on a golden barge.

Marion knew that Amelia played the harpsichord and she hoped to hear her play. Amelia greeted them and led Lady Winthrop to the best place in the room. Marion waited beside her, her heartbeat escalating when Amelia whispered that Lord Edgewater had arrived. She had not seen him since that disastrous evening at the Gold Room. Not that she wanted to see him, mind you, but . . .

A commotion at the door pulled her attention. She frowned with dislike when she recognized Sir Cedric. He seemed to be in his cups, weaving unsteadily across the floor. The oxlike butler, Smithers, followed closely behind him, and only at a word from Amelia did he remove himself. Sir Cedric found a place behind Marion, and she could smell the wine as he breathed on her neck. To get away from Sir Cedric's foul odor, she moved as far forward on her seat as she possibly could.

Lady Winthrop fanned herself, and turning around, said good evening to Sir Cedric. Marion pretended not to see him, but that didn't stop him from leaning over her shoulder and prattling inanities. She cringed but steeled herself. No word of complaint would pass her lips.

When the Earl of Edgewater arrived, Amelia made a show of introducing him to Lady Winthrop, then to Marion, as if it was the first time they met.

"Oh, my, you're the gentleman who took my niece's inheritance," Lady Winthrop said and sniffed. "I'm not sure that Marion—" She snapped her mouth shut, and Marion could see that she was struggling between a feeling of outrage and the titillation of being introduced to such a grand personage as the earl. "I'm not sure I should be talking to you, Lord Edgewater."

Marion gave the earl a glare, since she still hadn't forgiven him for the possibility of his selling off the land that should be rightfully hers. Papa had not sent a reply to her inquiry. The earl smiled—oh, ever so sweetly—then sat down beside Lady Winthrop. *With the older lady between them, he figured I wouldn't stab him in the side with a hatpin,* Marion mused, and told her heart to settle down. It didn't listen.

More guests arrived and within the hour the room was full. Fans fluttered, gentlemen cleared their throats, whispers sibilated. The orchestra tuned their instruments, and Amelia welcomed everyone. She settled herself at the harpsichord, its sides painted with gentle pastoral scenes so popular in the eighteenth century.

The frail metallic tune of the harpsichord filled the room, and the talk ceased. Marion threw a covert glance at the earl and noticed that the music had captured his entire attention. It was well performed, and she let herself be drawn into the fragile yet powerful minuet.

Amelia had hired excellent musicians. An hour that seemed as short as minutes quickly passed. As the last bar tinkled to an end, enthusiastic applause filled the room. La Naldi, who entered late with an entourage of admirers, sang three ballads and an aria, and at the grand finale she reaped ecstatic cheers.

There was a short pause, then Amelia, splendid in a golden gown and plumes in her hair, approached the earl. Marion leaned slightly forward to see what was happening. Amelia whispered in his ear, but he shook his head. She tugged at his arm and pulled him toward the harpsichord.

Speechless, Marion watched her friend push him onto the seat and set a sheet of music before him. He gave Amelia a murderous glance and argued in angry whispers.

Smiling, Amelia said, "I know that not many of you have heard the Earl of Edgewater play. But now we'll have the opportunity to enjoy his wonderful talent."

The earl's fulminating glare would have scorched Amelia if she'd been standing any closer. She indicated that he should start and sat down next to Marion.

A hush fell over the crowd. It was marred by a rhythmical snoring coming from Sir Cedric. The earl raised his fingers over the keyboard, then began to play, hesitantly at first, then with increasing gusto. Marion recognized the music as a piece by Johann Sebastian Bach. The earl never ceased to amaze her. It was rare to hear a gentleman play the harpsichord, since musical entertainment usually fell onto the shoulders of the ladies. He played very well, yet Marion sensed a reluctance in him.

She exchanged glances with Amelia, who winked. What devilry was going through her friend's mind, Marion wondered.

The music ended and the earl reaped a thunderous applause. Two red spots glowed on his cheeks, and Marion noticed that he was deeply upset.

The guests started milling about the room and footmen began moving away the chairs. Emily Ralston dragged her mother to where the earl was sitting at the edge of the crowd, and Marion noticed how the Incomparable cooed and clucked over the poor man. No wonder he didn't like debutantes, Marion thought.

She looked away, and the next time she glanced toward the earl he was gone. There was no sign of Amelia. Footmen brought around trays with refreshment, and Lady Winthrop accepted a glass of wine.

"I'm glad that dreadful tinkling is over," she said and took a deep gulp of wine.

"I thought it was quite good," Marion replied and accepted a glass of lemonade from a footman. A worry nagged at her. Where had the earl gone? She wished she could remain angry with him, but she found that the emotion had passed after seeing his discomfort as he left the dais.

Amelia finally joined them. "I hope you enjoyed my little entertainment."

"Very much," Marion said. Her eyes tried to ask Amelia where the earl was, but her friend turned to Sir Cedric, who again was hanging over Marion's shoulder. "Stronger beverage for the gentlemen is served in the next room." Before she could finish the sentence, the young man had left, and Marion drew a sigh of relief.

"Why don't you taste some delicacies at my buffet? I

shall order a footman to assist you with the plates,'' Amelia said to Lady Winthrop.

Lady Winthrop accepted gratefully. She never said no to delicacies as long as they came from someone else's table but her own. She always preached to Marion that ''thrift!'' was a divine virtue . . .

''Where did the earl go?'' Marion breathed to Amelia behind her aunt's back.

''I don't know. His hat and cane are still here, so he hasn't left the premises. You might find him in the library.''

''I don't know . . . I don't want to see him.''

Amelia's dark eyes filled with laughter. ''You're doing it too brown, Marion. I'll tell your aunt that you went upstairs to refresh yourself. I'll keep an eye on her and get her involved with the wags. Go.''

''Shall I challenge the earl?''

''It's probably too early for that, but perhaps you can play a friendly hand. There are cards on the desk in the study.'' Amelia pushed Marion toward the door. ''Go now.''

Marion ran out before Aunt Adele noticed that she had left. She quietly entered the library. Closing the door, she waited until her eyes had adjusted to the relative darkness inside, since the drapes shut out the last of the evening sunlight. She heard sounds of chatter from the garden, where some of the younger guests had gathered. She should be with them, not stalking some gentleman in a darkened room.

''Who's there?'' came a muffled voice from the leather sofa whose back was turned toward Marion.

Marion recognized the earl's voice. ''It's me, Marion.''

''What do you want?'' he demanded gruffly. ''Have you come to laugh at me?''

''No . . . I— I, well, worried about you. I came to congratulate you . . .''

He sat up abruptly and stared at her. "I thought you were angry with me."

"I—er, well, yes I am, in a way, but—" Her voice trembled and faded. She took a step toward him, and he beckoned her to sit down beside him. His hair was mussed as if he'd pulled his hands through it repeatedly.

"I only wanted to tell you—" she said in a rush. "I really liked your music. You played like a virtuoso."

He snorted with disgust, and Marion halted her progress toward the sofa. "That's a blatant plumper, stripling."

Marion shrugged, still uncertain what to do. "If you can't take a compliment for its face value—"

"Come and sit down for a minute," he said, sounding infinitely tired. He patted the tufted seat at his side. "Come here, I won't bite you."

Stiff as if she had a fire poker up her back, she sat down. She folded her hands demurely in her lap. "I didn't know you could play so well."

"Stop joking," he said. "I only dabble in music."

Marion heard the venom in his voice, and she gave him a long stare. "You ought to play more often. I, for one, would love to hear more."

"I don't want to talk about this, not now, not later. There's nothing more to say on the matter." He looked exhausted, dark rings encircling his eyes.

"What's wrong?" she asked.

He sighed, and it sounded much like a dry sob. "I can't damned well sleep," he muttered. "I'm so tired." He raised his head. "Sorry about the rude vocabulary."

"I don't want to pry, but why can't you sleep?"

"If I knew, I would dashed well sleep," he said with a lash of venom.

He sounded tense, on edge. He patted her hand in a paternal manner. "I didn't mean—"

"Why? What is worrying you so much that you can't sleep?" she demanded to know. Every day she learned more about this man who had touched her more deeply than she wished.

He looked at her steadily with red-rimmed eyes. "If you really must know, I feel as if I never do anything that *I* really want with my life, and it's eating me inside. The real me was shaped and pressed into this uncomfortable form called the Earl of Edgewater, a man I don't even like very much." He raised his hand as he saw her on the brink of protesting.

"Yes, yes, I do everything I'm supposed to do. I apply myself dutifully to my estates, the charities, the people who work for me. Everybody prospers. Yes, I certainly do my *duty*. You can ask Mother if you don't believe me."

"I do. I've always sensed a deep boredom in you, P—Pierce," she shuttered as she used his given name for the first time, without his permission.

"Look at you, Marion, you always do what you want, right in the face of convention. One day you might get caught and find your reputation ruined, but I give you the highest grade for courage." He tilted her head up so that he could look into her eyes. "If I had an ounce of your spirit, I would be a strong man."

"You are strong . . . and so capable, but what *do* you want out of life?"

"I would like—" He hesitated as if on the brink of a confession, then changed his mind. His mouth curved into a wicked smile. "I want . . . well, you."

She knew he'd been about to say something else, but before she could pry an admission out of him, he'd taken her face between his two hands and kissed her mouth. That swooning sensation that she'd felt at their first kiss came over her again. A hot wave of sensations rolled through her, and her skin seemed lit by an inner fire.

He relinquished his hold abruptly and dropped his head into his hands. "I didn't mean to embarrass you like this," he said hoarsely.

"You didn't," she whispered and touched her lips in wonder.

"You ought to leave, Marion. You've been here at least ten minutes, if not longer."

Marion did something she'd never dreamed she would do. She moved farther down the sofa, then beckoned him to place his head in her lap. Without as much as a second prompting, he complied and closed his eyes. Ever so softly, she stroked his hair and said, "You must listen to your innermost feelings. They'll tell you what to do."

His lips quirked at the corners, but he didn't open his eyes. "Like they do to you? I'm not sure I could have such a madcap life as yours." He sighed. "Marion, you're turning my life upside down, and I don't know if I can handle it."

She suppressed her urge to swat his head. "Mawworm. Don't pretend to be helpless," she whispered.

"But I am! Too many emotions are pushing to get outside, and I don't like it."

"Let them fly like the birds. When I was a child, my mother used to sing to me. She'd invent her own songs about cats and dogs and birds. She used to say that when one is happy, one's heart soars like a meadowlark." Marion hummed a tune. "You know, she had the loveliest voice. Mine isn't half as nice." Crooning a lullaby, she gently caressed his forehead. Within the minute, he was fast asleep. The calm, somnolent air made Marion sleepy as well, and her head tilted toward her chest.

A few minutes later, after what seemed an eternity, she was aware of a voice whispering her name. "Marion! Psst, Marion! Your aunt is looking for you."

The earl awakened with a jerky movement, and Marion blushed to the roots of her hair. "I've been sitting here innocently watching the Earl of Edgewater sleep."

"You've been gone for an hour," Amelia informed her. "Pierce, where are your manners? Have you lost all sense of propriety?"

The earl pushed his hand through his hair. "That's easy to do in the company of Miss Marion," he said dryly, "and well you know it, Amy."

Marion stood and brushed the wrinkles from the front of her gown. "Yes, blame it all on me!"

"Sir Cedric is also looking for you," Amelia continued. "He's in his cups, so I would stay away from him if I were you, Marion."

Fortunately, Marion thought, Sir Cedric had not made any advances toward her since she accepted his proposal—a small blessing in the chaos that was her life.

After giving the earl a self-conscious smile, she left the room with Amelia. For a moment, before she closed the door, his gaze burned hotly into her, and she knew that glance had changed the course of her life. She felt tingly all over and quite unable to speak.

"I say, Marion, you didn't have to let the earl—"

"I don't know what got into me. Let's not speak about it." Marion rapidly changed subject. "Anyway, nothing happened. I'm still as innocent as I was when I got here this evening."

Amelia scowled. "Hmm, I'm not so sure about that."

CHAPTER 12

THE FOLLOWING EVENING SIR CEDRIC ARRIVED AT ALBEMARLE Street to escort Marion to a ball at Ralston House in Grosvenor Square, a ball that had been talked about as one that would be the most lavish squeeze of the Season. Marion did not look forward to attending, but Lady Winthrop said she could not decline an invitation from the eminently fashionable Lady Ralston.

"Next to Emily, I'll look like something out of the ragman's bag," Marion muttered to herself. Dressed in a white gown that was slightly too big for her, she disliked herself intensely as she viewed her reflection in the mirror. The gown had a fussy row of yellowed white satin bows down the front, bows that had been salvaged from one of Lady Winthrop's old dresses. Marion contemplated removing them with a pair of scissors, but Pansy entered with the information that Sir Cedric was pacing a hole in the carpet downstairs.

"Dashed rum sort," Prinny commented from his perch in the cage. "Siiiirrr Bertram, Siiirrr Cedric," he continued. "Popinjay—jay—jays."

Pansy clapped her hands to her mouth, and Marion laughed. "He imitated your voice, Pansy."

"Well, I've never! I'm ever so embarrassed."

Marion wagged her finger. "You have to be careful what you say around that parrot." Her spirits buoyed, she stepped downstairs. Her aunt, who would not miss a ball at Ralston House for anything less than an earthquake, was resplendent in a puce taffeta edged with Mechlin lace, with a cluster of puce ostrich feathers in her hair. She gave Marion a swift, critical appraisal. "I suppose you must do. I wish that Pansy person would have found a way to tame your curls by now. She's been here for weeks."

"You know it's a hopeless cause," Marion said *sotto voce.* She gave Sir Cedric a bland smile as he bent over her hand.

"You're looking ravishing," he said, but Marion could tell he had difficulty uttering the falsehood.

"Let's not pretend," she said, and drew her lace shawl more closely around her. "You know as well as I do that you'd rather not be here."

He squeezed her hand so hard that her engagement ring of emerald and pearls dug into her tender flesh.

Ralston House was alight with hundreds, no thousands, of candles, Marion mused as she stepped into the circular foyer. The floor gleamed as if it'd been hand-buffed by a legion of maids, the prisms of the chandeliers sparkled like stars, rich velvet drapes swathed every window. The hostess, Lady Ralston, the jewel in this gilded setting, looked like a goddess in her silks and diamonds. Lord Ralston, the wizened little man beside her, was said to be one of the richest men in Britain. No wonder Emily Ralston was the debutante of the year, Marion thought. Not only had she beauty, but also fabulous wealth that drew suitors of all kinds. Emily only had her eyes set on one man, though, the Earl of Edgewater.

"Marion," she breathed when the Ralstons had greeted the Winthrops by the staircase that curved like a lyre up toward a dome that was painted more lavishly than the dome of St. Paul's. "I've been looking for Lord Edgewater. Did you see his carriage as you arrived?"

"No . . . As he's no friend of mine, I didn't particularly look for him. Why do you want to see him, Emily?"

"I had hoped he would come up to scratch, you know. He has been very attentive lately. I can't bear the suspense."

Marion unfurled her fan and remembered the glorious hour when he'd rested his head in her lap. Had she been wrong to believe that his kiss had held as much significance to him as it did to her? He'd said he wanted her . . . but she could not believe that. It was a fabrication of his smooth tongue. The possibility that he was only toying with her heart struck her. "I think he treats every debutante with equal if indifferent courtesy. He probably likes to crush as many hearts as he can before the Season is over. Some gentlemen find such sport entertaining."

"Oh, no, he's not like that," Emily sighed. "I so want to marry him! Isn't he the most handsome, most chivalrous, most—"

"You're exaggerating greatly," Marion said coolly.

Emily drew her breath sharply. "Oh, dear, forgive me. I quite forgot what he did to you, to your father."

Marion followed Emily into the ballroom and sat down on one of the spindly gilt chairs along the wall. "It's not so easy for me to forget."

Emily heaved another sigh, and her lips trembled with emotion. The dimple on the right side of her face deepened prettily, and Marion viewed it with envy. "But you must admit that he's the most—"

"I won't admit to anything, Emily. I don't know the gentleman."

Emily's eyes narrowed in speculation. "Of course . . . after all, you are engaged to be married to Sir Cedric. How did he ever persuade you—'' She studied Marion's emerald ring with interest. "I'd say it's worth—''

Marion snatched her hand away. "Emily, I don't want to discuss my engagement *or* the virtues of Lord Edgewater.''

Emily tilted up her Grecian profile in an attitude of affront. "Marion, I'm disappointed in you. I thought you would be my confidante; somehow I thought I could trust you even when other ladies look at me with hatred as I enter a ballroom. I thought you weren't like them.'' She arranged her pale rose silk gown around her, and Marion realized how lovely she was. Still, that classic beauty didn't make Emily any friends. In other words, Emily was as lonely as she was, Marion thought, stunned by that revelation. The witch and the princess. Suddenly she found the idea hilarious and started laughing behind her fan.

"Really, Marion, what did I say to make you laugh?''

Marion lowered her voice. "We are the witch and the princess. Beside me, your beauty shines more brightly.''

Emily smiled. "That was kindly said, Marion. I think I like you.''

"Of course you do,'' Marion murmured.

She couldn't believe she heard right when Emily added, "You're sweet, Marion. I don't know any nice people except my father.''

Marion saw beyond the trappings of wealth and found that Emily perhaps wasn't as empty-headed as she appeared in larger groups.

"Let's be friends, then.'' As they agreed to the friendship, Marion felt a newfound warmth inside. Emily left her side to dance with her father; then the ball was opened. Sir Cedric did his duty, dancing twice with Marion. Sitting next to her aunt, she then watched the various sets from the chairs along the wall. No one asked her to dance. She tried not to look at every gentleman who entered the ballroom, and she suppressed any feeling of disappointment when the earl did not arrive. Her life seemed to be in a vacuum, as if every logical thought was impossible. She kept hearing the earl's voice, seeing his smile every time she closed her eyes. Every one of her nerve endings were tuned toward his arrival. He must come! The thought of Emily winning him was unbearable . . .

Marion gasped. The realization came to her in a flash. She was in love with the Earl of Edgewater.

"Well, look, there's the pianoforte-playing earl and Mrs. Milford," Lady Winthrop said, breaking into Marion's thoughts.

Marion's head jerked up, and her breath caught in her throat as she recognized the earl.

"Not the thing for a gentleman to play a musical instrument like that."

"I thought he was very good, Aunt Adele."

"Irregular, nevertheless," Lady Winthrop said, fluttering her fan agitatedly. "I hear Miss Ralston is to marry him."

"He hasn't asked her," Marion pointed out, bristling.

"According to Lady Ralston, it's only a matter of time."

Before Marion could reply, Amelia sat down beside them. "Good evening, Lady Winthrop, Marion."

Lady Winthrop gave a curt nod. Marion realized that notwithstanding Amelia's connection to Lady Jersey, Lady Winthrop considered Amelia below her own station and a female of dubious reputation. No real lady would take up residence alone in her brother's town house without an older relative to supervise her activities. Never mind that Amelia was a widow and a lady very capable of taking care of herself. "No, I don't want you to fraternize with her any longer," Lady Winthrop had said after the musicale. "Mrs. Milford has too many opinions, opinions on all manner of subjects. No *lady* would surely know so many *worldly* things. Why, she speaks just like a gentleman!''

Marion chuckled as she remembered those words. Glancing repeatedly toward the door, she had hoped that the earl would pay his respects. No such luck. He was already surrounded by his hosts and their relatives, dowagers trailing hopeful debutantes. No wonder he was loath to appear at the Society functions, Marion thought.

Without the company of the earl, the evening dragged on. It was a ball like so many others, lilting music, a hum of voices, the swish of open fans, the rhythmical clicking of heels against parquet. Marion wasn't part of it, and she grew increasingly restless. She excused herself to her aunt, explaining she would refresh herself before the late supper.

She went in search of Amelia and found her in a salon at the back that had been converted into a cardroom for the older gentlemen who didn't care to dance.

A profound stillness reigned among the gamblers, and Marion sidled to the edge of the crowd surrounding a table in the middle of the floor. Standing on her toes, she peered between the shoulders of two men to see who was playing at the table. Her heart almost stopped with shock as she recognized Lord Edgewater. She pressed her hand against her heart to still its racing beat.

Lord Edgewater had an emotionless expression on his face. The only live thing were his eyes: cold, glittering steel as they rested briefly on his opponent, Sir Cedric Longpole. *Sir Cedric!* Oh, dear, Marion thought in dismay. What will happen next?

In her eagerness to be close to the earl, Marion elbowed her way to the front of the crowd. Nobody tried to stop her, and she linked her arm to Amelia's. Sir Cedric scowled as he concentrated on the game at hand.

''The stakes?'' she whispered to Amelia.

"A pound a point. I don't know why they're playing at such high stakes."

Marion gasped in wonder at the high stakes. Her gaze flew to the earl's face, gauging his expression. Seeing the hard set of his jaw, she knew he was determined to win. With casual ease he placed the cards on the table, relentlessly taking trick after trick.

Studying Sir Cedric's face, she noticed his perspiring brow and working mouth.

The card game soon held her attention. In no time she recognized the earl's mastery, just as Amelia had told her from the outset. Marion's heart sank. She would never be able to beat him, even though she had won many games of piquet.

The earl played his hand well, and he seemed to see through the cards of his opponent, which had a very disconcerting effect on Sir Cedric. As the tension mounted to an agitated pitch, the earl calmly spread out an array of court cards on the table, and Sir Cedric's eyes threatened to pop. He groaned. "Damnation! You're obviously out to ruin me!" he whined and called for a waiter. "Give me some brandy."

"Capotted, by gad!" one of the spectators exclaimed with relish. "Five rubbers to one."

"How far are they going?"

"Ten rubbers. Sir Longpole has lost plenty of blunt, to a tune of five hundred pounds already."

Marion lips formed a silent "Oh?" It was the first time she had witnessed such deep play, and she knew that Sir Cedric had pockets to let. How would he pay? Perhaps he was counting on paying with Uncle Bertram's money after the wedding . . . Yet gambling debts had to be settled immediately.

Her gaze glued to the earl, she wondered what kind of

man he was to gamble at such high stakes? And what was stirring under his set exterior? She had so many questions about him.

The next hand was dealt, and the tension escalated. Marion followed the moves eagerly, trying to read the thoughts behind the earl's stony facade as he played out his hand. As if feeling her gaze, he suddenly looked up. Their eyes met, a flash of recognition in his acknowledging her presence. Marion lost her breath and turned deliciously weak inside.

The earl won the last rubber, and Sir Cedric reluctantly handed him a promissory note. "I will pay you shortly. Then we shall have a rematch where I'll win it all back," he said ominously, and stalked out of the salon, his face red with fury. The din of voices rose once more to the ceiling, and clouds of smoke tainted the air. Marion, hiding behind a potted palm, looked longingly at the earl, but as soon as he turned his gaze in her direction, she fled into the next salon. She had to remember that she loathed him, even though her heart spoke otherwise.

Through the doorway, she saw him extricate himself from a group of gentlemen and walk in her direction.

Her only retreat was the dark terrace, the last place she wanted to face him. "Oh, dash it all!" she spat as she saw there was no other way out. She hoped his coming in this direction didn't mean he was searching for her. She huddled against the wall behind an abundant flowering vine. The door creaked and she saw his tall form outlined against the light inside.

"Marion?" his deep voice called softly. "I know you're out there. You can't hide from me."

Marion took a deep breath and stepped forward. "Me hiding?" she said flippantly. "What a cork-brained idea!" She laughed, a flat nervous sound. "I was only taking a breath of fresh air. Why in the world would I want to flee from you, pray?'' She glanced at him, grateful that the darkness concealed her scarlet cheeks.

He leaned against the balustrade, his teeth gleaming white in the light from the salon. ''I take it you were loath to see me.'' He crossed his right arm over his left, swinging the quizzing glass at the end of its riband.

With a rush of words, she said, ''I'm fearfully embarrassed after what happened . . . last time.'' Staring into the darkness, she waited for his scorn.

''Oh, I thought you only ran out here tonight to repeat that sweet moment,'' he said in a grave voice. ''The kiss, I mean.''

''No, I should not be speaking to you, not after I found out your treacherous plan to sell my land. And now I hear you're to wed Miss Ralston.'' Her eyes scanned his face to see any traces of repentance and noticed that he was smiling.

''How can you accuse me so unfairly, Marion? I told you the sale was only a rumor. I quite looked forward to seeing you again. Life has been unpleasant and tedious these last few days without your company. About Miss Ralston . . . it takes two people to get married, and since you won't have me, I don't see myself caught in parson's mousetrap in the near future.''

Her face brightened. ''Really?'' She bit her bottom lip as the truth of his words sunk in. ''I suppose you take me for a complete ninny and that my stupidity amuses you. I shouldn't speak about Emily Ralston.''

''Stupidity holds no attraction for me, so don't bother bragging that it's one of your traits,'' he said dryly. ''Now, what have you been doing these last few days since we last met?''

He doesn't know about my betrothal, she thought. "You haven't read the papers, then?"

He shook his head. "Should I have read something important?"

She nodded. "Yes . . . I've decided to marry Sir Cedric Longpole after all."

His gaze narrowed and he lowered his arms. "But you loathe him. You told me so yourself."

"That doesn't mean anything. Anyway, it'll protect me from marrying you."

He studied her closely. "Marion, how could you! Did our kisses mean so little to you?"

Marion steadied her ragged breath and clenched the balustrade until her fingers ached. "I owe you no explanations. In fact, I owe you nothing. What I decide to do is no concern of yours."

He grew still and silent. A painful tension rose between them, and Marion made a move toward the door. He fell into step beside her. "Very well, I bow to your wishes. Let's talk about something else. Amelia told me of your zealous efforts to become a cardsharp." His voice was cool and flat.

"Not a cardsharp, only sharp at cards."

He chuckled sarcastically. "I daresay I ought to tremble with fear. Are you going to challenge me?"

"If you wish, milord." She made her voice deliberately airy. "But as you used all your energy to destroy Sir Cedric, you might be much too tired to engage in another card game tonight. Besides, Aunt Adele would have one of her turns if I played cards with you."

He seemed to ponder her words. "Are you implying that I'm a weakling? I could possibly find a few ounces of strength if I'm pressed. However, Sir Cedric sank to the tune of one thousand pounds. What kind of stakes are you suggesting? I might not have the funds—"

"Fustian! Everyone knows that you're as rich as the Golden Ball!"

"Come then, let us return inside so that I can demolish you in a rubber of piquet." Marion noticed a mocking light in his eyes.

"You hold yourself in very high esteem, milord." She eyed him disdainfully. "If you think you can chide me in this way, believing that I'll lose, you are more conceited than I thought."

"You'll lose—it's as simple as that."

She glared at him. "We'll see about that."

He laughed softly. "Your temper goes well with your bonfire hair." He lifted his eyebrows at her searing glance.

"I—I detest you!" She clenched her fists in anger, longing to plant a blow to his jaw.

As she showed him to an empty table in the small salon right off the terrace, she recognized Amelia's gown in the doorway from the corner of her eyes. She winced under her friend's disapproving eye and negative shake of head. Yes, perhaps Amelia was right. This might be the wrong time to challenge the earl. Mayhap her skills were not honed enough to beat him, yet how could she back out of the challenge? It was impossible.

The earl's gaze glittered across the table, and she narrowed her eyes in calculation. Swallowing hard, she drew the first card from the stack on the table.

"Low. You deal first," he said, gently teasing her.

As she dealt the cards, the earl studied her intently. In his head revolved one thought. What was her game behind the game? The Laurel Manor estate? She hadn't told him anything. His concentration lay not on the cards, but on her face. He saw nothing but her sweetly curved lips, the skin as fresh as new cream with a delightful spatter of freckles. He'd always found people with freckles to be loyal and good-natured, he thought with a chuckle. His best friend through school had been sandy-haired and freckle-faced. And so many others over the years, good people all. He laughed at the thought, realizing how angry Marion would be if she knew what he was thinking.

''What's so amusing?'' she asked suspiciously.

''Nothing. What stakes, Marion?'' He smiled at her in challenge, and she swallowed covulsively. He smiled. ''A penny a point?''

''Yes . . . I suppose pennies are as far as I can stretch at the moment,'' she muttered.

''Forty-one,'' he began, lifting his eyes from his cards to her face.

''Equal,'' she said, wishing she could see through his cards. She also wished her heart wouldn't pound so, making her quite confused. What she needed was a clear head.

They announced the combinations and the scores, and began playing out the hand, each summing up each other's skills. Marion won the rubber, and Litton whistled with appreciation. ''Have I met my match in a mere stripling? Much too embarrassing to even contemplate,'' he commented, tapping his fingers on the baize-covered table. A diamond on his little finger shot fiery sparks.

In silence Marion watched as he shuffled the cards and dealt out a new hand. This time she was sure he was holding back a high combination only to confuse her game, but what else could she expect? After a cat and mouse game, the earl won the rubber.

''Capotted, my dear Miss Marion,'' he announced, staring with exaggerated gloating at all the tricks in front of him. Marion felt a strong urge to wring his miserable neck.

They agreed to play a deciding hand, although the earl's points were well above Marion's. She dealt, waiting for his call.

The sounds of laughter and chinking of glasses from the adjoining salon disturbed her concentration, and she failed to remember the cards that had been discarded. What cards did he hold in his hand? She called a heart, and he chuckled.

"No, a spade is what I have. You're capotted and repiqued." He lifted an eyebrow. "Care for another hand?"

Embarrassed, she glanced at Amelia who had joined them. "Edgewater, how deuced ungentlemanly of you to win over such a charming lady. Besides, are you trying to ruin her reputation?"

"She thinks I'm selfish and uncaring, so this unorthodox behavior is just a confirmation of that," the earl said on a chiding note.

"I challenged him," Marion said and rose, "which was singularly foolish of me. I'm sure he has never had an easier game. I'd better join my aunt before she finds me here and causes a commotion with one of her fainting spells."

Tears threatened to choke her, but she stubbornly dismissed them. The last thing she wanted to do was to cry in front of him. The whole silly episode was her own fault, after all. Turning her back on the earl, she bent to retrieve her fan from the seat of a chair.

"You're still the unvanquished master, milord."

He laughed. "And I hope to be for a long time. Can you imagine how wounded my pride would be if you had managed to fleece me?"

She whirled toward him with a heated retort on her tongue, but when she saw the grin on his face, she could not help but laugh. "Oh, how very vexing you are!"

His appreciative glance swept over her. To her chagrin, she blushed, much too aware of his scrutiny. What had changed since that first kiss? Her heart.

"If I spend more time with you, the tattlemongers might

whisper that I have designs on you. I've behaved quite ungentlemanly.''

''No harm done,'' Marion said airily and moved toward the door. ''No one but Amy saw us.''

Amelia, closely behind her, tut-tutted. ''You'd better behave, Marion. I'll take you back to your aunt.''

''A young miss must be careful whom she chooses as gambling partner,'' the earl said behind Marion. ''If she wants to win.''

His words made Marion wish she were five years older. ''It's rude to speak of a lady's age, Lord Edgewater, no matter how . . . young,'' she retorted heatedly.

''Put my foot in my mouth, did I?''

''Constantly.'' Marion turned toward him in the doorway. ''You're overbearing, insufferable, milord, and I regret the day I became involved with you.''

''It was night, remember?'' He shifted his gaze to Amelia ''Amy, don't look so grim.''

''You're monopolizing Miss Marion, Pierce. One could almost think you're having designs on my friend.''

''Wholly innocent, I assure you.''

Marion wanted to scream that she wasn't a young girl any longer. She was a woman with a woman's feelings. ''It's none of your business what I do, Lord Edgewater,'' she said with a toss of her head.

''Since you're so eager to see me go—'' He bowed smoothly, then took himself off, only stopping to speak with Lady Ralston at the door before leaving the premises.

''You know it was too early to challenge him, Marion. You could not but lose.'' Amelia fanned herself vigorously.

''Yes, a foolish thing to do, but he teased me something dreadful.'' Marion's gaze wandered aimlessly over the assembly, the ladies in their glittering dresses chatting amicably. Her gaze was caught by the piercing gray eyes of an imposing woman dressed in a pewter-colored dress, plumes adorning her dark and silver-streaked coiffure, and three strands of pearls gracing her neck.

Marion whispered under her breath. "Who is that lady. She's staring."

Startled out of her thoughts, Amelia scanned the room. She breathed, "That, my dear, is the Dowager Countess of Edgewater, Pierce's mother. Do you want me to introduce you?"

Marion's heart jolted with sudden fear. "Yes . . . well, no. I . . . don't know."

"Don't be shy, Marion. She looks like she would like to meet you."

Amelia dragged her toward the ballroom doors. "Lady Edgewater, may I present my good friend, Miss Marion Rothwell."

"Ahh, the Somerset Rothwells. I'm delighted to meet you, Miss Rothwell. I've met your father on a number of occasions. I heard about his failing health, and I'm sorry." Her eyes twinkled warmly, and Marion relaxed. There was something about the other woman's face that reminded her of the earl.

"You know about my . . . er, that I'm acquainted with your son?"

"You must be, since he's involved in this tedious business about your inheritance. It was most unfortunate." She shook Marion's fingertips. "I hope to see you at one of my tea parties soon, Miss Rothwell. I'll be sure to send you an invitation." With a wide smile, she left.

"She was pleasant," Marion said to Amelia.

"Yes, she's very loyal to her friends. You could do worse than cultivating her acquaintance."

"If you don't mind, I would like to find my aunt and

leave. I have a blinding headache, and my spirits are low after losing to the earl.''

''That's understandable. One of these days you'll win, and I'll be the first one to cheer when you recover your inheritance.''

CHAPTER 13

THE FOLLOWING AFTERNOON SIR CEDRIC SENT IN HIS CARD TO Aunt Adele, who was supervising Marion's work in the library at Albemarle Street. Marion was reorganizing the books under the letter N, and it was a time-consuming task, indeed! Face dusty and her hair awry, she read the print on the stiff cream card over her aunt's shoulder. "I wonder what he wants," she said suspiciously.

"Surely he's eager to spend as much time as possible with you," Aunt Adele ordered Fawley, the butler, to send in the young man.

Sir Cedric bowed to Aunt Adele and gave Marion a veiled glance. Marion wished she knew what he was thinking. "Good morning, Lady Winthrop," he said with his most ingratiating smile. "I see that I have chosen an inconvenient time to visit."

Aunt Adele donned the affected airs of a tragedy. "Not at all, Sir Cedric. You're always most welcome in this house, and Marion was so looking forward to your visit."

Marion cringed and glared at Sir Cedric. He gave her an empty smile in return, which made Marion think of the expression of a dead fish.

Aunt Adele continued, "However, I might not fulfill my hostess obligations in a satisfactory fashion, be it that I have the most debilitating sick headache this morning. And working among these dusty books gives me an unpleasant tightness of breath.'' She fanned herself and opened and closed her mouth repeatedly.

''It distresses me no end to witness your obvious discomfort,'' the young man said and kissed Lady Winthrop's hand extravagantly. ''Is there anything . . . ?''

Marion made a face at him behind Lady Winthrop's back as he continued his bland, insincere expressions of sympathy.

''I appreciate your kind offer of support, but at this point no one can help me,'' Lady Winthrop said laboriously. She sat down, leaned back with her eyes closed, and flung a limp hand over her brow. Only two minutes ago she'd been fit as a fiddle, Marion recalled, giving orders like a drill sergeant.

Lady Winthrop made a sudden recovery. ''Is there anything we can do for you, young man?''

''In fact, I'm here to invite Miss Rothwell for a drive in the park. My curricle is waiting outside.'' He motioned to the littered desk. ''Would that be acceptable? I don't want to interrupt important work.''

Aunt Adele gave a faltering smile. ''How very kind of you, to be sure.'' She turned to Marion. ''Do adjust your hair and put on your hat and cloak, Marion. And don't make your fiancé wait indefinitely.''

Even though Marion had no desire to drive in the park with Sir Cedric, any outing would be better than cataloging books.

''Thank you, Aunt Adele.'' Marion left the desk, the catalog cards scattering around her and the ink drying on the tip of the quill. Heedless of the mess she abandoned, she opened the door. Sudden, hysterical parrot laughter echoed in the hallway outside.

"Damnation!" shrieked Prinny from above. "Siiirr Cedric. Cooome here. Coxcomb!"

Sir Cedric looked startled, and his Adam's apple wobbled above his neckcloth. "I say! That parrot is growing increasingly rude. I used to find him delightful, but now, I don't know . . . How did he know I'm here?" He gave Marion an affronted glare. "Prinny's not very polite to me. I don't believe he's moving in with us when we've tied the knot."

Neither am I, Marion thought, suppressing her laugh as she ran upstairs. Prinny must have overheard her calling Sir Cedric a coxcomb. That parrot had more sense than most of the people she knew.

When Marion returned, Sir Cedric said, "You look ravishing, Miss Marion. Like a delicate flower in full bloom."

"Rubbish! Don't construe such blatant untruths, Cedric. It doesn't suit you." After taking a hasty farewell of her wilting aunt, Marion walked before him to the front door. She unfurled her parasol against the glaring sun and let Sir Cedric assist her inside the curricle.

"Do you like the new color?" he asked. "I just had it painted."

Marion looked at the yellow wheels. "Yes, very dashing. You're up to all the rigs, Sir Cedric. I daresay my uncle paid for it."

Sir Cedric was visibly taken aback. "I don't know what you're talking about, Miss Marion. Ladies don't talk about money. When we're married—"

"I would like to have you know . . ." Marion bit her tongue. She couldn't jilt him, not yet. First she would have to win back Laurel Manor. "Perhaps . . ."

"What are you talking about?" He jumped onto the seat next to her and took the ribbons.

"Nothing."

In silence he tooled the equipage south to Piccadilly and turned toward Hyde Park. Within the gates, fashionable vehicles crowded the lanes, and Sir Cedric nodded and waved at his acquaintances.

"Tell me, Cedric, what induced you to gamble with Lord Edgewater last night?"

Sir Cedric turned to her in agitation. "How do you know about that? A lady is not supposed to know about these things."

"I was there, and I watched as you lost one thousand pounds. How do you plan to pay such a large debt?"

Sir Cedric stiffened. "That is none of your concern. Besides, I'll regain my losses at the rematch that's bound to happen shortly."

Marion noticed the perspiration beading on Sir Cedric's forehead. It was obvious that he worried about that coming event. She felt a twinge of compassion for him, but it didn't change her dislike. Sir Cedric only wanted her for the paltry ten thousand pounds that Uncle Bertram would pay him upon the event of their marriage. "I wouldn't gamble with Lord Edgewater if I were you. He's bound to fleece you."

"Don't tell me what to do, Marion!" he snapped. "You're taking orders from me, not the other way around."

Anger flared to life inside her. "Is that so? We're not yet leg-shackled."

"But we'll soon be, and then—"

"Then what?" Marion had difficulty suppressing her wrath, but she didn't want to create a scene in public.

"By the way," continued Sir Cedric, "I think we ought to get wed right after the banns, the very first day afterward."

"You mean move it up a week? Why the hurry?" Marion demanded, her hand tightening on her parasol. She knew very well why he was prompting her to accept an early wedding. The money reward.

Sir Cedric licked his lips repeatedly. He seemed to be working himself up to a confession. The horses could feel the tension and skittered nervously. Sir Cedric sawed on the reins in vain. ''I . . . you mean so very much to me, Marion, so very much, I can't wait.''

''Gammon, Cedric. You don't care a fig for me, nor I for you.'' The truth slipped out before she could stop herself. Still, Cedric already knew her feelings.

''That's vastly unfair, Marion. You don't know what goes on in my heart.''

''Greed,'' Marion said without blinking.

He hissed something that sounded very much like a curse. At that moment, one of the horses had decided it'd had enough abuse to its tender mouth. As a rook swooped over its head, it bolted, egging the other steed into following. Before Sir Cedric could react, the horses had set off at a dangerous pace. As the carriage wheel bounced into a pothole, Marion lost her grip on the seat and was tossed to the ground.

She heard screams, then her body smashed against the turf. As pebbles dug into the palms of her hands, she lost her breath for a moment, then the scent of earth and dust clogged her nose. She slowly faded, only vaguely aware of the sounds of voices and the thudding of steps around her. She felt no pain, only a spinning sensation in her head.

''Are you hurt?'' some stranger asked, and inserted an arm under her shoulders.

She forced her eyes open and saw a sea of worried faces above her. ''What happened? Are the horses safe?''

''The rig is halfway around the park by now and slowing down. Deuced thoughtless of the driver—''

"What's going on here?" someone's voice boomed. A constable knelt beside her as she struggled to stand up.

"I'm whole," Marion said and brushed off her cloak.

A phaeton came to a halt at the edge of the throng. "Miss Rothwell? What in the world happened?"

Marion looked into the kindly face of Lord Edgewater's mother. The dowager stepped down, and the crowd parted. She took Marion's arm.

"I'll survive, Lady Edgewater. No broken bones."

"You come home with me. I'll send word to the doctor and to your uncle at Albemarle Street."

Still in shock, Marion felt too weak to protest. The constable helped her into the phaeton, where a gentleman friend of the dowager assisted her onto the seat. The dowager placed a rug over her knees and a comforting arm around her shoulders.

Marion felt quite recovered as they reached Hanover Square. The butler assisted her inside, and Marion forgot her adventure as she stared at the lovely octagonal hallway. Oak wood paneling and marble floor gave the entrance distinction. A stairway soared toward the thirty-foot ceiling, disappearing into a long corridor above. Huge paintings of illustrious Edgewater forefathers adorned the walls of the staircase. Six doors led from the foyer to who knows how many salons. Marion inhaled the subdued air of elegance and wealth.

"The rose salon, Griggs," ordered the dowager.

"This way, miss," said the butler and led Marion toward one of the doors. She sank down on a rose-and-bone-striped sofa and eyed the many gilt frames, the airy refinement of porcelain statuettes, oriental urns filled with sweet-smelling lilacs, the elaborate baroque plaster mantel piece. "What a lovely room," she breathed. "I wish I had a home to call my own."

The dowager smiled and discarded her hat and cloak. Underneath, she wore a pale lemon empire-style gown with a puckered muslin yoke that formed a ruffled edge around her throat. "I'm glad you like it. It has taken me a lifetime to arrange it just the way I like it. As you must understand, it's not easy to coordinate heirlooms handed down from collectors of all previous epochs. But I'm quite pleased." She rose and spoke with the butler at the door.

"I've sent a message to your uncle," she said as she returned. "Who is your doctor?"

"Please don't bother. I don't need a doctor. I'm perfectly recovered."

"You must at least stay for tea," the dowager said, and went to a bellrope.

"Thank you, I would enjoy that." Still a bit shaky, Marion leaned back against the needlepoint pillows.

"I'm glad to have the chance to know you better, Miss Marion. I'm sure you don't hold this family in high esteem since the matter of Laurel Manor." She sat back down and patted Marion's hand. "I assure you, however, that my son is not an ogre."

Marion hesitated. "I . . . know. I'll find a way to regain my inheritance from him."

The dowager's elegant eyebrows rose a fraction. "I'm intrigued. How are you going to do that?"

Marion hesitated, then looked away.

The dowager laughed. "You're afraid I'll give the strategy to Pierce?" When Marion nodded, she continued. "I assure you, I'm not a spy for my clodpole son."

Marion's laughed. "Oh, no, Lord Edgewater is not a clodpole. I reserve that epithet for Sir Cedric Longpole. Today was a good example of his 'clodliness.'"

Lady Edgewater laughed. "I must agree that he was

somewhat of a blockhead letting his horses bolt like that. Still, not all gentlemen hold the ribbons with a light hand.''

Marion hastened to add, ''I don't want to speak ill of Sir Cedric. There are better things to discuss.''

''Is that so?'' The dowager settled back against the pillows at the opposite end of the sofa, spreading her skirts around her. Her eyes danced with mirth. ''Well, then you'll have to help me find a suitable epithet for my hopeless son.''

''There are no names bad enough for *him*,'' Marion said with a toss of her head.

The dowager laughed. ''Upon my word, I have never encountered such impudence!''

''I wonder what he would say if he overheard me,'' Marion said with a smile.

''I wonder. He needs someone spirited like you to shake him out of his doldrums.''

''Doldrums?''

''Yes, the poor man has these bouts of insomnia, and they always make him very low.''

Marion's heartbeat escalated as she recalled that brief hour when the earl had rested his head against her lap and fallen asleep.

''He struggles with some problem. He has for a long time, but he won't confide in me.'' The dowager heaved a dreary sigh. ''I don't know why I'm telling you this, Miss Rothwell.'' Shaking her head, she gazed speculatively at Marion. ''There is nothing anyone can do to help him. He struggles with his demons alone.''

The butler entered with a tea tray and set it on the table. Marion watched the dowager fill paper-thin cups with the golden tea and received hers with a nod of thanks. The butler handed her a plate filled with cucumber sandwiches, cream puffs, and buttered scones. Marion realized that she was quite hungry.

"There. That will be all, Griggs." The dowager waited until the retainer had left the room before she turned to Marion with eagerness. "Now we can enjoy a comfortable coze. You mentioned your lack of home, and I declare my son has been very ramshackle not to return Laurel Manor to you."

"He did, but I refused to accept it. I'm sure he won the estate in fair play, and the fault lies entirely with my father, who let it go with a snap of his careless fingers." Marion wrinkled her brow. "I don't understand it. Papa was very proud of the old heap of stones. He invested my dowry into Laurel Manor." She tried unsuccessfully to suppress the tremor in her voice.

"Hmm, I believe Pierce might be willing to part with the estate if you challenge to win it from him."

"I know. I already thought of that. I'm going to beat him at his own game—piquet." She clapped her hand to her mouth. "Oh, dash it all! You won't tell him, will you?"

"Indeed not!"

Marion drank deeply from her cup to steady her nerves. Talking about her present situation was daunting to say the least. She lived a day-to-day existence with the Winthrops, who were eager to see her go. The dowager's interest in her gave her untold support, a feeling of warmth that she hadn't felt for years.

The dowager pondered Marion's words in silence for a few moments. "To beat Pierce at piquet might be a bad strategy. He is too good at it; in fact, I believe no one has bested him at that game for a long time. Perhaps you should find another way." She gazed frankly at her guest. "Do you know any other games?"

Marion's eyes filled with astonishment. "Any other

games? Of course. I'm rather proud of my skills at chess. But if you mention to Lord Edgewater that I'm knowledgeable of such a game, he'll instantly take me for a bluestocking." She gulped down her tea as that thought made her agitated. It mattered a great deal what the earl thought about her.

"Are you a bluestocking?" the dowager queried as a smile curved her lips. She nibbled daintily on a cucumber sandwich as she watched Marion.

Marion nodded and blushed. The dowager had a knack for making her bare her soul. "If loving books makes me one, I am. Still, I . . . don't want the earl to dislike me. He's not as 'evil' as I thought from the outset. In fact, he's thoughtful and kind."

"Your affection for my ramshackle son moves me." A softness tinted the dowager's voice, making Marion swallow hard.

"He's not ramshackle in the slightest. He's been my constant support, although I confess I was very furious with him at first for taking my inheritance. The only question that puzzles me is why he seeks my company."

"You're refreshingly honest. Pierce hates any form of deceit. That's the one major reason that has kept him from marrying some nubile young lady. The schemes of the debutantes and their mothers have made him quite set against marriage. I'm sure he doesn't feel threatened by you."

"No, he treats me like I'm his ten-year-old—*sister*," Marion complained.

"And you have more . . . er, adult feelings toward him?" The dowager's eyes lit up, and Marion squirmed under her kind perusal.

"Eh . . . I don't know—exactly. He's an accomplished flirt." She swallowed the remains of a scone, then placed her napkin with finality on her plate. "I daresay I have trespassed on your hospitality much too long already."

"Oh, no, I quite enjoy your company. Furthermore, you haven't seen the library yet." The dowager reached for the teapot. "And now, I'm going to tell you a secret. I'm glad you divulged your interest in books, because I have the same 'weakness.'" The dowager refilled their cups. "In other words, I'm a bluestocking."

Marion stared at her hostess with dawning admiration. "You are? Who would have thought . . . Well, I've never! When I confessed my partiality to books at the beginning of the Season, my fellow debutantes suffered fits of the vapors. My popularity dwindled into nothing. Not that I was that popular to begin with—"

The dowager chuckled. "I find you highly entertaining. You used the wrong tactics informing your 'friends' so quickly about your love for the written word. It's better to listen and to wait; someone is bound to share your interest." She tapped the side of her teacup with her fingertip. "Miss Rothwell, with a little more polish, you could easily outshine the others. And with your literary knowledge, you could maintain an interesting conversation with your dance partners. Nothing bores a gentleman more than vapid smiles and fluttering eyelashes. They like an entertaining companion, someone who can share their secrets, their dreams, their lives. No real man wishes to be saddled with a whining female who dares nothing, and knows nothing."

"You're wrong! They *do* like vapid smiles and fluttering eyelashes." Marion sighed. "But I rather wish I could gain such style as you possess."

"Why, you sweet girl!" Laughter poured from the dowager's lips. "But you're exaggerating. You know, you've already set your mark on the *ton* by introducing that fiery red hair of yours."

"Amelia Milford said the same." Marion stared gloomily out the window. "No, Lady Edgewater, I've lost my battle against drabness. I could never acquire style."

"Nonsense! Please call me Dot, short for Dorothea. These long names and titles are so very tiresome." She smoothed some crumbs from her gown. "The battle is never lost unless you give up."

Marion listened to her hostess's words. "I believe you're the wisest person I've ever met."

The best of friends, they walked out of the sitting room. A footman held the door to the library, and they entered the room made cheery by warm wood paneling and a small crackling fire. First, Marion noticed the gleaming pianoforte, and she wondered if the earl spent hours playing his music here. Then her gaze flew over the walls lined with books, and she gasped. "Your library is well stocked, indeed. It would take a lifetime to study all these."

"My favorite room, y' know. I would dearly enjoy a game of chess, but my son will be back soon. Since no one has come to fetch you, he shall drive you home." She went to one of the shelves. "You must choose a book to take with you. That will create a reason for visiting me again, and then we'll have more time to get to know each other. Perhaps you could try to best Pierce at chess and win your estate back."

Marion studied her hostess closely. "I'm surprised that you could face your son's potential loss of Laurel Manor with equanimity."

Dot laughed. "I should say that to *you*. You have lost everything that is dear to you. If I can help you relieve some of your distress, I'll be very happy. Besides, Pierce has plenty of worries without another estate to look after." She patted Marion's arm and pulled her toward the books.

"I shall win back my estate soon from Lord Edgewater and return home. There I can indulge in reading as many books as I wish, and no one will chide me for my spectacles and my hair. But, I assure you, I will beat the earl at his own game of piquet, not chess.''

A doubtful look stole into the dowager's eyes, but then she brightened. ''Perchance times are changing,'' she commented, ''he's bound to lose some time.''

Marion slid her hand across the leather-bound backs of the volumes. She pulled a title from the shelf, eagerly leafing through the pages.

''Milton? Yes, very romantic, but I prefer Lord Byron's poetry myself,'' the dowager said, perusing another slim volume. In comfortable silence they became engrossed in the pages. They both started with surprise when hearing the earl's deep voice by the door. ''Just what I thought, absorbed in abstractions.''

Marion's heart hammered wildly, and heat stole into her cheeks. She glanced shyly at him, meeting his calm gaze.

''Good afternoon, Lord Edgewater.'' She drew a sigh of relief when she saw no disapproval in his eyes.

''Miss Rothwell, I heard about your mishap from Lord Exton, who drove you two home from the park. Wait until I get my hands around Sir Cedric's neck.''

''Heavens, such show of emotion!'' the dowager said dryly. ''Pierce, you must escort Miss Rothwell to Albemarle Street. My abigail will accompany you as chaperone.''

''I have quite overstayed my welcome,'' Marion said and cradled the book in her arms.

The dowager walked across the room with a rustle of skirts. ''You may keep the volume and bring it back here sometime soon. I enjoyed your company, Miss Rothwell.''

Marion smiled with pleasure and bobbed a small curtsy. ''My pleasure entirely, and please call me Marion.''

Outside, the sun shone warmly, announcing that spring had really arrived. During the trip back to Albemarle Street,

Marion spoke dreamily to the earl. "What a wonderful woman your mother is, Lord Edgewater. I rather think my mother was like her. Unfortunately, I didn't know her well, as she died when I was ten."

"Mothers can be quite a handful, but I can find no fault with Dot. She goes her own ways and leaves me alone. How was your life with your father?"

"Good, I suppose. He's never had any sense about Society and the Society rules. I think he was happy to cart me off to Aunt Adele. At first, the Winthrops showed no reluctance to bring me out, but the tune changed when they saw what I looked like. I declare Aunt Adele had one of her Spasms when she first clapped eyes on me. They had not seen me since I was an infant, and *all* infants are pretty. She wanted to make me dye my hair black, of all things."

The earl gave her a long, penetrating glance, which Marion returned breathlessly. "Odd, to be sure," came his comment at last, and Marion was too dazed to know if he meant the adoration in her eyes or the talk of dyeing her hair.

She played with the fringe of her shawl. "You would like my father."

"Have you already forgotten the infamous game?" he asked dryly. "I've been acquainted with Horace Rothwell for some time. Although he didn't often come to town, he always created quite a stir when he arrived. A flamboyant, congenial man."

"Yes, and very kindhearted. People often took advantage of his generosity." Marion felt a rock of sadness weighing her down. "But Papa is not like he used to be."

"He was foolishly rash."

Marion sniffed. "I already know that! You don't have to remind me. I love my father dearly."

"Give him some time. Perhaps he will recover all his faculties."

Marion had no desire to think beyond the present moment. She was only aware of the earl's knee pressing deliciously against hers. Ultimately her heart had betrayed her. She was in love with the enemy. Did he read the truth in her eyes?

CHAPTER 14

To Marion's relief, she'd found that Lady Edgewater's abigail, Hopper, was hard of hearing. Perhaps the dowager had sent that particular servant so that Marion could speak freely with the earl in the carriage. She didn't put it past the dowager to meddle, a trait that Marion didn't particularly like. At the same time, she was grateful that she could speak without fearing gossip among the servants later. She didn't want the old maid to hear her next words.

"Lord Edgewater . . ."

"Call me Pierce."

"Pierce, your mother mentioned your bouts of insomnia. Haven't you found out why yet?"

The earl laughed derisively. "Did she tell you that I had scarlet fever and croup as a child as well? Did she give you my whole life story?"

Marion smiled in embarrassment. "No . . . I don't mean to pry." She sensed the warmth of his smile as he sat on the opposite seat of the barouche.

"That's exactly what you're doing. I can't think of any other name for it."

"Oh, desist teasing me! I *am* interested in your past. You've told me nothing about your father."

The earl's sigh was heavy, and Marion sensed his

hesitation. "Father adored the word 'duty.' He always did what was expected of him. He ruled the estates with meticulous discipline. In his mind were no shades of gray, only black and white. He was an exceptionally strong man who cast his shadow everywhere."

"You don't sound too enthusiastic about him."

"He gave me a very firm upbringing. I was to see no shades of gray, either."

"But you do," Marion said in a low voice. "That's what's bothering you, isn't it? You feel guilt because you're not like him."

"By Jove, aren't you the perfect mind reader?"

"No . . . but you must agree that you differ from him."

The earl heaved a deep sigh. "You have to dig to the bottom of this, don't you?" When Marion didn't respond, he continued. "I could never live up to his expectations. He's been dead five years, and I can't shake off his influence. I won't be half the man he was."

"Only because you like to play the pianoforte?"

The earl jerked forward and gave her an angry glare. "How do you know about that?"

"I noticed the pianoforte in the library, and don't forget that I heard you play the harpsichord at Amelia's house. You're very good. Your music gave solace to my soul. Why deny that gift?"

Some tension left him, and he leaned back against the squabs. "S'faith, do you really think I'm good?"

"Yes, and I think it's a sin to waste such a gift. Not many can play as well as you do. You must not throw away such a talent."

He shot a glance at the abigail beside Marion as if gauging if he dared to voice his next statement. Evidently he deemed it safe as he took a deep breath and continued. "I like to play many of the old masters, but my true interest lies in writing my own scores.''

''They, why don't you do it?''

''Gentlemen don't play the pianoforte; they might play the flute, but they certainly don't write music.''

''Mr. Handel did. Your father stopped you from playing, didn't he?''

The earl nodded. ''He said that I'm to live by the code of the Littons, not chase some dreams that will ultimately bring disgrace to the family name.''

''You must not listen to his ghost any longer. You shouldn't deny your inner longings for music, or your life will be empty. Why, you told me yourself that you often get bored. Running the estates are not enough, don't you see? You have to fulfill your dreams.''

''You have a lot of gall, Marion, daring to tell me that I'm conducting my life wrongly.''

''But you are!''

''The estates take up much of my time; I have no time for frivolous music.''

''Those words are straight from your father's mouth. You must be happy; that's the only way to live.'' Marion's cheeks grew hot when she realized that he could make her happy by telling her that he loved her. But no, he only sat silent, pondering her words. His next statement startled her out of her reverie of love.

''Since you're so vehement about my dreams, what about your own? What do you expect out of life? Marriage to Sir Cedric, a man you don't love?''

''I . . . don't . . . I mean my uncle forced me into it.'' Marion fought an urge to divulge her decision to jilt Sir Cedric, but something inside prevented her from speaking frankly. ''I must obey him.''

"I thought Sir Cedric wanted your inheritance, not you—"

"And now that I have nothing, why would he marry me?" Marion could not stop the vitriol from lacing her voice. "Why, indeed? I have nothing to inspire passion, do I?" She felt his eyes on her, but she looked away. "I called him toad-faced. What do you think he calls me? The cobra with hair that would make a gentleman cry."

The earl chuckled. "I haven't heard any rumors to that effect, but you never know."

"Oh, you!" Marion couldn't abide his chiding voice. "Don't you dare laugh at me!"

"The part about the cobra was good, but I don't know about the hair. I quite like it the way it is."

"Stop teasing me. I don't wish to speak about myself."

"But you don't mind prying into my deepest secrets." The earl's voice had taken on an edge, and Marion wished she'd never started the conversation.

"My hair is hardly a secret," she said. "Neither are my spectacles, or my general ugliness." She gave the offending wire-rim frames a decisive push up on her nose.

His voice gentled. "I think you're the only person who believes that."

I wish you would tell me that you love me, she thought. *I wish you would find me desirable, lovely. I wish so many things . . . but they are only foolish dreams.*

"Silent? You, Marion, speechless?"

"I was woolgathering."

"I thought you might change your mind and marry me. You implied as much to your father," he pointed out.

"I wasn't formally engaged to you; I never considered myself tied to a promise." She sighed. "Anyway, our association will soon be over—once I've regained my estate."

"I had hoped that we could remain friends, but since there's no guarantee that you'll ever retrieve your lost inheritance, we'll probably end up enemies before this is all over."

"Cold and calculating," she murmured, "just like your father."

"That was a low blow, Marion."

"All is fair in war and . . ."

"Love." His eyes glittered wickedly as the coach came to a halt in front of the Winthrop torch-lit front steps. "We've arrived. I'll help you down and deliver you into the caring hands of your aunt."

"No need to do that. It's enough for her to know that I arrived home." As one of the footmen opened the door, she said a subdued good night and fled inside.

The next morning Sir Cedric arrived at Albemarle Street in a great state of agitation. "I must speak with Miss Marion at once," he said to Lady Winthrop, who deigned to welcome him from her general lookout point, a chaise lounge by the window of the blue salon. Bolstered by an enormous mound of pillows, she viewed him from an opening in the many layers of her cashmere shawls. Marion, only dressed in the thinnest of muslin morning gowns, bent deeper over her embroidery, stabbing the canvas with gusto.

"You were careless yesterday, young man," Lady Winthrop said. "Very careless. My niece could have died, you know."

Sir Cedric paled. "I'm awfully sorry." He gave Marion an entreating glance. "May I speak with her?"

Lady Winthrop waved a weary hand. "Take her to the library. But only five minutes mind you, Sir Cedric."

"Yes, of course." He took one nervous step toward Marion. "Are you ready?"

Marion followed him reluctantly. She didn't need his profuse excuses, but it did him credit to show such concern. The library smelled of old leather and Uncle Bertram's sweet hair pomade. Marion sat down on the leather sofa and cradled a pillow in her arms. "Why do you want to speak with me? You've been forgiven. You couldn't know the horses would bolt."

"Thank you," Sir Cedric said. "However, the accident is not the issue here."

Marion tensed, giving him a probing glance. "What do you mean?"

"You spent the entire evening with Lady Edgewater, and then the earl drove you home." He bristled with anger, his face flaring an angry red.

"My, haven't you been busy prying?" she said, standing. "There's no reason for us to discuss this further." Filled with alarm, she headed toward the door, but his next words halted her progress.

"Don't fly into a pet, Marion. I won't allow you to consort with the Littons. Why, the earl stole your inheritance. How can you be on friendly terms with the enemy?"

He did have a point, Marion thought, but the sweet memory of Lord Edgewater's kisses could not be suppressed. "The dowager worried about me after the fall. She acted in an entirely proper way. Anyway, you can't tell me what to do. I'm not your wife."

"Why didn't she take you straight home?" Sir Cedric took a step closer, and Marion feared that he would try to force his embrace on her.

"I don't know why she didn't drive straight to Albemarle Street. I was too dazed to notice. Still, I was happy to make the dowager's acquaintance. She's a very interesting lady."

Sir Cedric balled his hands into fists. "Marion! I forbid you to be associated with Lady Edgewater."

"Don't get into high fidgets, Sir Cedric. What has she done to offend you?" Marion realized that fear was making Sir Cedric raise his voice.

"Nothing other than that she's associated with Lord Edgewater. Despite his lofty title, he's nothing but a common cardsharp, a cheat."

Anger came to life in Marion's chest. "Cheat?" she said with lively disgust. "He won the card game fair and square. You're upset because he bested you at Lady Ralston's ball."

Sir Cedric took another threatening step toward her. "You stay away from him, do you hear? When we're married I shall teach you how to behave. I won't accept any of your cheek." He caught her to him, and she pushed against him.

"Let go of me! I'll scream."

He tried to plant a kiss to her neck. In a blaze of fury, she kicked him hard in the shin, and he let go for a moment. She rushed to the door. Breathless, she halted on the threshold. "I've had enough of you, Sir Cedric! I'll go to my uncle right now and cancel the wedding." She realized that would be a mistake before she'd sorted out her own affairs, but Sir Cedric had goaded her into this announcement.

"I'll never marry you, Sir Cedric."

Not waiting to see his reaction, she slammed the door behind her. She rushed up to her room wondering how long she would be able to keep this news from her uncle. Until she'd been able to win back her estate? Hardly likely.

CHAPTER 15

"Miss Rothwell is delightful, don't you think?" Lady Edgewater asked her son as he returned home after delivering Marion to Albemarle Street.

"Hmmm, yes, I suppose she is, but also irreverent, inquisitive, domineering, and brash."

"I would rather use the words original, interested, frank, and full of *joie de vivre.*"

"You're entitled to your opinion, Mother. I take it she found great favor with you—after all, you have all those qualities."

Lady Edgewater slapped the earl's wrist, then poured him a cup of tea. "You must admit that she's charming."

The earl pondered the word. Marion was more than charming; she was intriguing, entertaining, and adorable. He realized that he'd almost adopted her as one of his family; he felt responsible for her. It really mattered what happened to her. "I know that she's going to be married to Sir Cedric Longpole in two weeks."

The dowager studied him above the rim of her teacup. A teasing light shone in her eyes. "That must try you sorely."

"Me? Why should it?"

"I thought you cared about Marion."

"I do, but I don't govern her life. Still, I think Sir Bertram is making a big mistake in forcing Marion to marry that fortune hunter, Sir Cedric."

"You can't call him a fortune hunter now. Marion has nothing but her clothes, and as far as I can tell, her wardrobe isn't worth much."

"Even without her estate, she's a woman who has a richness of spirit," the earl muttered and set down his teacup. He stood. "Good night, Mother. There's no need to speculate about my feelings for Marion. I like her. Very much." He bent over his mother and kissed her cheek.

As he left the room, she called out. "Marion, Lady Edgewater, the sequence has quite a ring to it, don't you agree, Pierce?"

"Devil take it, Mother. I'll order you back to the country."

"Humbug, you'll do no such thing!" As he closed the door, the dowager stood and smoothed her gown. "I think I'll take Miss Rothwell under my wing. Where match-making mamas have failed, I shall succeed."

Marion worried that her uncle would hear that she'd jilted Sir Cedric, but he'd said nothing at supper time. Sir Bertram only talked—with some animation—about the upcoming wedding, which would be held in a small chapel not far from Albemarle Street. The coming Sunday, the third banns would be read, and the house was abuzz with servants cleaning for the approaching ceremony on the following Monday. Sir Cedric had not returned to speak with Lord Winthrop, so he knew nothing of Marion's plans. Nervous about the outcome of the ordeal ahead, she spent every free hour with Amelia, training her skills at piquet.

Amelia had, in Marion's honor, invited a small group of people, Lord and Lady Winthrop, Melvin, Lord Edgewater and the dowager, and Sir Cedric, to a dinner party with card games rounding off the evening. She had written a note to Lady Winthrop that pointed out how much a lady of such indifferent health as herself needed a break from the preparations of the upcoming wedding. How readily her aunt agreed, Marion thought. The Winthrops were coming to the big night when she might make a fool of herself, or once again find herself the owner of Laurel Manor. So be it . . .

The day before that dinner party, Amelia announced that Marion was ready to challenge Lord Edgewater.

"I can't thank you enough for your support," Marion said and hugged her friend. "Lady Fortune smiled upon me the day when I met you."

Amelia gave a ripple of laughter. "I've enjoyed our friendship immensely, and I look forward to seeing Pierce's long face when he loses."

"If he does," Marion said darkly, and left Amy's house.

Elated that the end of her waiting was near, Marion stepped into Hookham's library on the way home. As she entered the door, the familiar scent of dusty books assaulted her nose. Her gaze darted along the shelves and soon alighted on Lady Edgewater, who was bent over an open volume of poetry.

"What a delightful surprise," the dowager said. "I sent a note over to your house this morning to invite you to tea."

"I didn't know—I've been engaged elsewhere."

"You'll come to tea, though, won't you?" The dowager propelled Marion out the door. "I have something I'm dying to show you, Marion."

"Tea? Who else is invited, if I may be as bold to ask?"

Dot smiled. "Just you and me. Pierce won't be there. Does that disappoint you?"

Marion shook her head, hiding her chagrin. "I'd much rather discuss poetry with you than argue with him."

Dot linked her arm to Marion's. "I have the most splendid idea. You'll see when we get home."

As soon as they reached the mansion in Hanover Square, the dowager gave orders about tea. Marion discarded her hat and cloak, and the dowager led her to the salon where they'd had tea once before. After pulling the bellrope, she asked Marion to make herself comfortable. The dowager carried an air of excitement, and Marion looked at her curiously. The older woman sat down and took one of Marion's hands into her own.

"Marion, I've taken a great liking to you. I would like to speak with you on a slightly . . . personal level, if you don't mind."

Marion frowned in suspicion. "I'm not sure—"

"Please hear me out." The dowager took a deep breath. "It's quite obvious your aunt won't move a finger to rig you out in style, dear Marion, and I'd love to do that for you. In fact, you would be doing me a favor to accept my offer." Her face beamed with anticipation. "You know that I never had a daughter of my own. I wish I had one to bring out, someone like you."

"Anything you do won't make me look any different."

"You're wrong! I'd like to show the world what a beauty is hidden under all that unkempt hair."

Marion pondered Dot's words. She was too surprised to speak for a long moment. "How could I ever accept such generosity? I could never repay you."

"Nonsense! As soon as you've recovered your inheritance there will be no questions of funds. Shall we start today? Of course we'll have to be careful and not do too much at once. If we start now, I promise you'll be the new Incomparable the next Season."

Marion caught some of her friend's exuberance. "I warn

you, Dot, you'll have your hands full.'' She pointed at her nose. ''These freckles don't fade.''

''It doesn't signify in the least. Come, I have already made an appointment with Monsieur Gerard to cut my hair, but instead he shall cut yours.''

Followed by Marion, Dot hurried out of the salon just as the butler arrived with the tea trolley. ''Bring the tea to my private parlor, Griggs.''

Marion said as they climbed the stairs, ''Aunt Adele will notice the change and wonder how I managed.''

''Ah! Well, tell her the truth. There's nothing she can do about it. She can't make your hair grow out again. You may tell her you happened to meet me and that I insisted on your company at my appointment with the hairdresser. He fell in love with the color of your hair—and so on.''

''She'll be displeased.''

Dot snorted. ''I will speak to her if she as much as tweaks your nose. Don't dawdle! We don't have the entire day.''

Upstairs, in Lady Edgewater's boudoir, the hairdresser, who had no more than two strands of hair to call his own, was already waiting. His expressive face lit up as soon as he laid eyes on the two ladies.

''Ah, Leddy Edgewotter! Yo need new 'air arrangement, *ne c'est pas*?''

''Yes, Monsieur Gerard, but today we must cut this lady's hair into a becoming style.''

''*Oui, la petite* needs a new coiffure urgently.'' He bustled forward with an oily smile on his lips and brandishing scissors above his head. ''Lovely *couleur!*''

Marion could not help but smile at the enthusiastic little Frenchman.

Half an hour later she was speechless when she saw the miracle he'd wrought with his comb and scissors. Sitting in front of the mirror of Dot's dressing table, she watched her bird's nest hair leave room for a cap of fashionable short soft curls delicately framing her face. The small, unremarkable features of her face that had always been hidden by her hair now showed to their advantage. Marion could only stare in awe. "This is not me," she breathed.

"You are a wizard, Monsieur Gerard," Dot said, evidently pleased with the transformation of her protegée as she clapped her hands in delight.

"*Voilà, très bien. La Petite* is bootiful, a little bird with copper feathers." He waved his arm about in a theatrical fashion. Sweeping off the cape covering Marion's shoulders he packed his case and rushed to the door. "Many *appointements,* he said in apologetic tones, and left.

"Absolutely splendid, Marion. Who could have guessed your mop of hair hid such beauty? You will make all the other debutantes green with envy when they see you."

"I have no desire to awaken such feelings in the bosoms of the poor ladies. However, there's little risk of that." Marion spoke with much feeling.

"Balderdash! I know of one person whose attentions you wouldn't reject." A teasing smile played over Dot's lips.

"Who?" Marion blurted out, her indifference instantly evaporating.

"Pierce, of course. I have noticed the warm glances you send in his direction." Dot spoke kindly and placed an arm around Marion's stiff shoulders. "I think he'll adore your change of style." She gave a whoop of mirth. "Indeed he will!"

"I must be a source of constant amusement to you."

"Please don't be miffed with me, Marion, but my dearest wish is to see Pierce's eyes light up with love. I have yet to meet the woman who will kindle that light in him, but I believe you have as good a chance as any. Pierce is a blind fool, but I think he already has a soft spot for you." She touched one of Marion's gleaming curls. "With a little push in the right direction—who knows."

Marion wondered silently if the kisses she had shared with Pierce were any indication. He'd kissed her as if he couldn't help himself. To her, his lips had tasted of heaven. A wave of delicious warmth rolled through her at the memory.

"You must not have heard about my nuptials to Sir Cedric Longpole. The wedding is on Monday morning."

The dowager grew quite still. "I'd forgotten." As if all breath had left her, she slumped for a moment. The exhilaration was gone. Marion thought of confessing the truth—that she'd jilted Sir Cedric—but she couldn't do it. Anyway, Sir Cedric seemed to think that the ceremony was still going to happen, since he hadn't informed Sir Bertram of her decision. Perhaps he didn't believe that she had the nerve to confess the truth to Sir Bertram.

The dowager regained her aplomb. "Never mind! You'll look lovely at your wedding, and that's what counts."

Marion sat down on the comfortable peach-colored sofa and noticed yellowed sheets of music on the table in front of her. She studied the scores but didn't recognize any of the music.

"What's this?" she asked the dowager. "Are you studying music?"

The dowager shook her head and walked to her wardrobe, slowly opening the door. "No . . . I found those in the attic this morning. I believe Pierce wrote that music some years ago. I meant to show them to him, but I forgot."

Marion put aside the music as Dot opened the wardrobe and pulled out a dress swathed in a protective cloth. Pushing aside the cover, Dot held out a creamy silk dress for Marion's inspection. "The empire style with its high bodice suits your form to perfection. And with your long, slender neck, you'll look lovely in pearls.'' She fingered the lace edging on the bodice. ''You must admit that this will suit you much better than the sacks your aunt insists you wear.''

Marion instantly liked the shimmering gown that was eminently elegant in its simplicity. ''It's too much—''

''Don't sit there staring like an owl, Marion. Put it on.'' Dot handed her the dress and placed herself on the chaise lounge with an air of anticipation. ''I can't wait to see the transformation of you into a fashionable young lady.''

''I can't possibly—''

''Of course you can! I won't hear any more protests from you. This is but a small gift from me, and remember what pleasure it will give me to see you dressed in a way that befits your station.'' She paused for breath. ''You wanted to look stylish and confident—well, this is a small step in the right direction.''

Marion could not argue with that barrage of arguments. As Marion began to unbutton her old gown, Dot rang a bell, calling the abigail from the adjoining dressing room. ''Hopper, please help Miss Rothwell with that dress.'' She pointed at the gown that she'd spread on the bed, and Hopper obediently began to undo the row of buttons at Marion's back.

The silk caressed her like a second skin, and Marion could not believe the transformation the simple dress brought to her. All of a sudden she looked like any of the young debutantes who had never suffered the humiliation of being a wallflower at the balls. She felt fragile, uncertain, but as she moved, the stylish gown gave her youthful grace. ''Oh, Dot, I look so—so different—almost pretty.''

''Just as I suspected you would. You look ravishing, Marion. I wish Pierce were here to see you now.''

Marion silently agreed with her. Would he stop seeing her only as a friend, or was that an empty hope on her part?

"Aunt Adele will have one of her turns" was all she said and slowly swirled around in front of the gilt-framed glass.

"I'm sorry to say this, Marion, but your aunt lacks all the niceties."

"She did not use to be so calculating and frail, but Uncle Bertram is not an easy man to live with. He influences her, and he's very tight-fisted. He didn't want to spend any funds on a new wardrobe for my Season in London."

Changing the subject, the dowager said, "How I wish Pierce were here to admire your transformation." Dot stood and linked her arm through Marion's. "But you'd better return home before they report you as missing. I shall send over a few more gowns and walking costumes later." As Marion started to protest, she raised her hand to stem the flow. "And don't you say another thing. I can easily afford a hundred new gowns if I wish." She proceeded to plant a kiss on Marion's cheek.

"How can I ever thank you?"

"Don't mention it for one moment. You've brightened my day considerably, and that's all I could ask." The smile on her face faded. "If only you weren't marrying that dreadful Sir Cedric! I wish you were my daughter-in-law."

Marion blushed with embarrassment. She wholly agreed with Dot on that score, but she couldn't confess her true feelings. Soon enough, Pierce would notice her transformation—and then, who knows what would happen? She would meet him soon, at Amy's dinner party.

Amy had said that the time had come to challenge Litton at piquet. That she would. Before Marion left the mansion in Hanover Square, she tucked the music sheets under her cloak.

CHAPTER 16

AMELIA'S DINNER PARTY WAS A GREAT SUCCESS. EVEN THOUGH THE Winthrops looked askance at Lord Edgewater, whose presence reminded them of Sir Horace Rothwell's defeat, they could not prevent themselves from being dazzled by him—an *earl* no less. Marion watched with some amusement as her aunt preened in front of her new acquaintances. She bore no trace of the sick headache that had plagued her earlier in the day.

After the ladies had finished their coffee in the sitting room and the gentlemen had drunk their port in the dining room, the two groups came together.

"I thought a quiet card game would be just the thing to end the evening," Amelia said. She looked resplendent in a narrow red silk gown, a strand of diamonds glittering around her neck, and plumes in her hair. "In fact, the footmen have set up some tables in the library."

The guests agreed heartily, and Marion's heartbeat accelerated with anticipation. Lord Edgewater came to her side in the pandemonium of choosing partners for the tables. "I was quite taken aback when I first saw you this evening, Marion. I thought I saw a vision of loveliness, and then I recognized you." A smile lurked at the corners of his mouth.

"Took you by the surprise, eh? You didn't think I could look anything but frumpy?" Marion poked his arm with her fan in mock outrage, but warmth curled around her heart. His gaze lingered appreciatively on her form, and for once Marion didn't feel an urge to hide. She felt happy and beautiful, and she couldn't remember the last time those emotions had buoyed her. Her cheeks grew hot as she read something that wasn't quite innocent in his eyes. He seemed to devour her.

"Your mother is very clever. She's the one who suggested this transformation."

"Beware of Mother; she'll subtly rule your life, with the lightest of feathers and the sweetest of smiles. Only later will you discover the iron behind the softness, but then you're trapped."

Marion snorted. "Much reverence you show toward your parent!"

She was separated from the earl and forced to play a dull hour of silver loo. Due to Amelia's prompting, partners changed, and Marion knew she was trying to maneuver her into a game with the earl.

Marion rose from the table, sending a questioning glance in Amelia's direction. Her gaze fell on the earl, who stood at the edge of the group, his arms folded over his chest and an amused smile playing over his lips. She swallowed convulsively, overwhelmed by a warm surge of love. His eyes burned into hers, leaving her breathless. She relived the memory of their lips touching, of his hard body pressed against hers. She steadied herself against a table, tearing her eyes from his face.

"Marion," Amelia cried out. "Do you want to form a table with Pierce and Sir Cedric? Or challenge someone if you dare?"

That was her cue, and Marion's legs began to tremble

with tension. "I can beat any one of you two gentlemen," she responded with studied calm. Her heart hammered wildly, and her palms grew clammy. She had no wish to be the center of attention, especially when she had so many thoughts to sort out in her mind.

"I don't mind a challenge," said Sir Cedric with a sneer. "What do you know? Nursery room games?"

Her heart sank, and her smile grew stiff. "I know all sorts of innocent games, and I know piquet."

She heard her aunt's gasp, but she refused to look at her. Surely it wasn't bad *ton* to play a hand of piquet with one's fiancé . . .

"Piquet?" Sir Cedric chided. "You're taking on airs, my dear, but I'll show you."

Marion sensed the double meaning of his challenge. His pale eyes traveled down her face to her trim figure. She shivered with a wave of apprehension and disgust. "Very well, to win over you should be easy enough, Sir Cedric," she said with a lightness she didn't feel. Her legs threatened to give out as she sat down at the table. She glanced up, noticing that the earl had made his way to her side. He winked in encouragement, but Marion's stomach still churned with worry. She caught Sir Cedric's mocking eyes on her, and she braced herself to the ordeal ahead.

"Marion?" said Lady Winthrop in a faint voice. "Are you sure this is the right thing to do?"

Uncle Bertram muttered something malevolent under his breath, but Lady Edgewater had soon convinced them that an innocent game among family and friends was not a *faux pas*.

"You will regret the day you challenged me, Sir Cedric," Marion said loudly, her voice brittle with tension. She saw him pinch his lips together into a thin angry line. With a snort, his eyes fell to the cards on the green baize. Marion shuffled the deck. After such an intense period of practicing the game, she thought cards would grow out of her fingertips.

She found herself surrounded by the guests, and she vowed she wouldn't lose. The atmosphere was thickening with every rubber, and she was doing unexpectedly well. Evidently, Sir Cedric could not tolerate to be beaten by a female—his intended, to boot. His eyes flashed with anger, his breath becoming more labored after imbibing several glasses of brandy in rapid succession.

Managing to win two hands in a row, his self-importance reared its fat head, and he seemed confident of winning the rest of the rubbers.

Marion showed no emotion on her face, but her knees were shaking so violently she thought everyone must surely hear her kneecaps knocking together.

Sir Cedric might have managed to even the score had not his eagerness to win befuddled the strategy of his game. Calculating his cards wrong, he lost the last and deciding rubber to Marion. She saw it coming and struck before he knew what had happened.

''By Jove, Miss Marion won,'' the earl said in surprise, and a round of applause burst forth. Marion drew a breath of relief. Amy appeared at her side. ''Do it now; it's your only chance,'' she whispered. ''Challenge Pierce and force him to stake Laurel Manor. If he wins, you have lost nothing. At least you'll have the knowledge that you did your best.''

''I wonder what he'll ask in return,'' Marion whispered as Sir Cedric rose.

''You shall regret this, Marion.'' He eyed her darkly, then stalked from the room. The other guests were still watching Marion as she stood. She glanced at the earl, who was twisting the cord of his eyeglass between his fingers.

As he noticed her stare, his eyes narrowed in speculation.

"I would like to ask the undefeated champion of piquet to step forward. Lord Edgewater," Marion announced, "I challenge you to a game."

All eyes turned to the earl, who dropped his quizzing glass. Cocking his eyebrows, he scanned the assembly. "By Jupiter . . . of all the wonders in the world—"

"You cannot let that challenge go unanswered, Pierce," said the dowager.

"'Pon rep, are you going to let a female mock you thus?" commented Melvin Winthrop. "Show her who is the master."

The earl took a step forward, and the dowager clapped her hands enthusiastically. "Show him, Miss Marion!"

He stood in front of Marion, looking down into her eyes. As she sat down, he rubbed his chin thoughtfully, and understanding dawned on her face. "You will be sorry you challenged me, Marion." With an enigmatic smile, he lifted the tails of his coat and calmly sat down at the table. A lackey brought a fresh deck of cards and a brandy bottle for Sir Bertram, who was protesting loudly about the card game. Amelia filled his glass to the brim, a move that mollified him. Then everyone's attention was focused on the table.

Marion felt faint with nerves. She couldn't take the strain much longer. Her love for the earl had made it hard to challenge him. How was she going to live through this night? she wondered.

With all the calmness she could muster, she met the earl's gaze across the table. His expression had turned predatory, and she shrank in her chair. Only the memory of Laurel Manor had the force to make her straighten her back and put her fear away. She would regain her inheritance from him tonight. All she needed was concentration; she *would* win, she told herself.

His voice grated softly on her nerves when he spoke. "And what are your stakes, Marion? I hope they are higher than the heap of pennies you have at your elbow."

"Naturally," Marion responded too quickly. *Idiot!* she told herself. *What does he want, and what else do I have to stake?*

"The lady should ask first, Pierce," someone said.

A smile flitted across the earl's face like the flickering flame of a candle. "Of course, how very remiss of me. Well, Miss Marion, what do you ask of me?"

A hushed silence fell in the room as all waited expectantly for her demand. She took a deep breath and plunged in.

"I would like to have Laurel Manor in Somerset if you lose, Lord Edgewater."

"Ahhhh" surged from everyone's lips except the earl's. He studied her with an amusement that didn't quite reach his eyes. "That's no small request."

"You can well afford it, milord." Marion dug her nails into the padded seat of her chair. "What do you wish from me if I lose?"

Utter silence descended once more. The earl leaned back in his chair and unhurriedly toyed with his eyeglass. He waited until the tension became unbearable, until the crowd was ready to tear him to pieces if he didn't speak.

"I want your hand in marriage."

A gasp, like a violent gust of wind, went through the guests. "Shocking!" Lady Winthrop breathed and fainted into the nearest chair. Amelia rushed to her side. Marveling at his gall, Marion stared fixedly at the earl.

Sir Bertram thrust his head down and wove unsteadily across the floor toward the earl. "Now listen here, young man!"

Lady Edgewater hurried forward to intercept his angry

charge. She soothed him with soft words and a pat on his shoulder, then led him to a chair across the room.

Marion noticed that Sir Cedric had returned. He was livid with fury, his fists clenching and opening. She knew the earl had deliberately asked for such a stake to enrage Sir Cedric, since there was no love lost between the two gentlemen.

"I accept," Marion said in a husky voice, her cheeks so hot she thought she could heat the entire mansion on a cold winter night.

"This grand commotion can ruin the healthiest of concentrations," the earl mused. His eyes glittered with amusement, and Marion drew up her slight form. "Is this one of your tricks?"

"Of course not. This is deadly serious to me."

"Very callous of you, Marion, to wish me to lose face among family and friends." He spread out his long fingers on the table and flexed the joints. "I will make it difficult for you, remember that!" he added.

Marion's spirits sank, and she watched him hold out the deck of cards toward her. Her hand trembled slightly when she reached out and took one, lower than his. The earl's deal.

"Show Pierce a lesson he'll never forget," Amelia encouraged Marion while fanning Lady Winthrop's pasty face.

"You can't let yourself be bested by a female, Edgewater!" said Melvin. "I would put a pony on you, if there was betting."

The first of six rubbers was tight, but Litton won, as he did the second hand. Marion's nerves rolled into tangled knots, and perspiration pearled on her forehead. She felt Amelia pinch her arm lightly, a gesture that urged her not to give up. When Marion thought she had understood his strategy, he changed tactics, and she had to strain her mind to the utmost to follow his maneuvers. To fool her he held back valuable cards, deliberately losing tricks to make her confused.

Marion conjured up all the various advice Amelia had given her during the weeks of training. Dash it all if she would let the earl win! Her whole future lay in these cards. Now she understood how her father must have felt that night when he lost Laurel Manor, although she would never be as foolhardy as to wager her life's work at an evening of cards.

"Capotted and piqued, Lord Edgewater," Marion announced, her voice filled with triumph. She had managed to win the third hand. Two to one, and she had to win the next hand to make it even.

Wiping her palms absent-mindedly on her gown, she picked up the cards. She raised her eyes and noticed that the earl had seen her nervous gesture. The corners of his lips curled upward, and an unholy light danced in his gray eyes. He could always read her like a book, and Marion wished at that moment she had more polish, more guile.

The earl's long fingers closed around the brandy snifter beside him and he downed the amber contents.

"Do you need brandy to calm your nerves, Pierce?" Sir Cedric chided. "Afraid of losing to a lady?"

The earl's lips parted in a sudden smile. "Miss Marion is a better player than any of you. I consider it bravery on my part to accept her challenge." The diamond on his little finger flashed sparks of fire as he placed a card on the table.

Through narrowed eyelids he studied Marion. It was easy to see her nerves quiver, creating a sheen of perspiration on her translucent skin. A jolt of pleasure struck him every time he watched her, and to his surprise, he realized he wanted her—physically. A powerful need to take her in his arms, to trail the slender column of her neck with his tongue, overcame him. How could a chit barely out of the schoolroom have such an impact on his senses. What was the irresistible allure of her? He concentrated half-heartedly on the cards in his hand, willing her to win. But it wouldn't do for her to suspect that he wasn't playing all his strategies. Still, she was good, damned good!

Marion threw her last cards on the table. "Capotted, piqued, and repiqued," she cried triumphantly, and the spectators—all except Melvin—clapped.

"Dead even! Come, Pierce, you'll have to do better than that," Amelia cried out. "Another hundred points to go."

The heat from the many candles, the tension in the onlookers, nearly suffocated Marion, and she thought she could see the air crackle across the table. The earl's eyes held a suggesting caress, and Marion's breath caught in her throat. Expectant, she studied every tiny nuance of feeling on his face, those harsh planes that so reluctantly gave away any emotion.

The earl won the next game, scoring high points, and Marion's gaze blurred in vexation as the court cards danced in mockery on the green blaize. Biting her teeth together, holding her breath, she took a daring chance in the following game and managed to win. Even, again.

"You have to play a deciding hand," Melvin roared. "Dashed good sport!"

Marion knew that a heavy responsibility to win rode on her slender shoulders. If she lost, she would be unable to face her relations again. She pushed that thought away. Better deal with that scandal later. A scandal it would be sooner or later. Her gaze scanned the room and alighted on Sir Cedric's blotched face. Outrage and fury exuded from every pore of his rigid body. He meant to cause trouble, of that she was sure.

Her gaze flickered to the earl's smooth fingers as he deftly dealt the cards. Sweet warmth threatened to overcome her, befuddle her mind, but she resolutely barred any emotion. Her whole existence was at stake here.

"Let us see Pierce grovel at your feet, Miss Marion," Lady Edgewater said with a laugh. "What a triumph it would be for us ladies if you win."

The earl made a face and Marion ground her teeth. She met the earl's smiling gaze across the table. These were the most important minutes of her life.

In a toneless voice she announced the combinations and the scores and began playing out the cards. What cards was he holding back this time, she wondered, wishing the cards were transparent.

"I have no intention of losing this game," the earl declared calmly. "This is highly entertaining."

"Damned you, Edgewater! Only deep play can dispel your boredom," Sir Cedric said in a voice harsh with venom.

The earl leaned back in his chair, his cards protectively against his chest as he lifted his eyeglass to study Sir Cedric. One long, icy moment passed, and the prattle in the room died down.

"I never refuse a challenge, especially when it comes from a lovely lady," he responded coldly.

The setdown had the power to jolt Marion out of her fragile concentration. Would Sir Cedric go for the earl's throat? Someone placed a restraining hand on Sir Cedric's unyielding shoulder.

Marion failed to remember what cards had already been played. She gnawed on the inside of her lip. What were his last cards? She could scream with annoyance. Calling a diamond, she studied him tensely, feeling a rivulet of perspiration rush along her spine. Nothing on his face gave away his emotions.

"Wrong color, Miss Marion," he purred, rapidly scooping up the trick. Frozen in a moment of agony, Marion waited for the ax of defeat to fall.

"A spade." His words cut into her, as her gaze fell jerkily to the one card left in her hand.

Unbelievable.

"I have a heart. You have lost the rubber, Lord Edgewater." Marion's voice trembled, and she had to press her fingers to her temples to steady herself. A sunburst of happiness flared within. She had won! Laurel Manor was hers.

A thunder of cheers erupted around her. She found herself lifted to her feet by the dowager. "You did it! Good girl."

Amelia ordered bottles of champagne, and by the time the glasses had been poured, Lady Winthrop had revived enough to celebrate. Sir Bertram had celebrated enough; his head lolled against the back of a chair, giant snorts erupting from his mouth.

Marion grew embarrassed at the attention paid to her. At the other end of the room she saw Lord Edgewater raise a glass in salute, an enigmatic smile playing over his lips. An irresistible pull made her cross the floor. Fanning herself vigorously, she spoke.

"I pray your disappointment isn't gnawing a hole inside." She burned to trail a finger along the harsh plane of his cheek, to touch his lips with her own, but she did nothing.

"I'll survive, even if my ego has taken a knock tonight. May the best player win—without concern to fragile egos. I will have my solicitor draw up the papers tomorrow."

The earl devoured her flushed face, the sparkling eyes, the trim waist, the rise of firm bosom. *Child, woman,* what are you doing to me, he thought, wanting to wipe his palms on his thighs to deaden the longing in his hands to touch her. It was no use denying the clamor in his heart. He urgently wanted to bed the sprite. Disgusted with himself, he drawled. "You have taken the title of champion with storm. Congratulations."

Marion sighed. "Thank you."

Silence hung uncomfortably between them. Marion shifted her weight to her other foot and studied him. Then she blurted out, "Did you *let* me win?"

She watched his features soften, but could read no affirmative answer on his face.

"I daresay you won all by yourself, stripling. You have become a real cardsharp."

Marion felt her skin grow hot as his gaze dipped lazily and lingered at the edge of her bodice. If it was deliberate, she might never know. "Wo-would you have—collected your prize if you'd managed to win?"

Her gaze hung on his lips.

He toyed with the stem of his champagne glass. "Most certainly! A bet is a bet." He smiled. "It would have been a most delightful upheaval."

She placed a hand on his arm. "In a way, you didn't lose."

He frowned, and she perceived a slight stiffening of his stance. "What do you mean?"

"I'll never marry Sir Cedric, and I told him so in no uncertain terms." She lowered her voice. "However, my uncle doesn't know yet, and I want to be far away when he finds out."

The earl whistled under his breath. "I'll be blowed."

Marion had no further interest discussing her future prospects with him. She fetched her reticule, out of which a roll of papers protruded. "I'd hoped for a quiet time to give you these." She handed him the roll. "But there won't be another chance tonight."

''What is it?'' He eyed the yellowed papers with suspicion.

''I wish to hear these some day. In fact, I shan't speak with you again until you promise to play for me.''

''My old music scores!''

''Your father perhaps didn't want you to play, but he doesn't rule your life any longer. I wish you would return to the work that can give lightness to your heart and dispel your boredom.'' She cocked her head to one side. ''If you return to your music, I'll bet you won't suffer from insomnia again.''

''You have a lot of gall, Marion. I don't know how many times I've told you that.'' He tucked the roll of music under his arm. ''But I might listen to your advice, or I might not. You have a sensible head on your shoulders.''

Nothing could have made Marion happier. Love was more than a soaring sensation in her heart; it was caring, and helping.

Their absorption in each other was disrupted by the sound of heavy doors slamming and the ruffled appearance of Smithers, the butler. His nose was bloodied, and Amelia was already hurrying toward him to find out what had happened.

''Th' cove planted me one,'' the burly man grumbled.

''Poor Smithers, who is no lightweight, had to carry the brunt of Sir Cedric's fury,'' the earl said under his breath. ''Your fiancé is angry, indeed.''

CHAPTER 17

"I LOVE HER," PIERCE SAID TO THE DOWAGER ON THE FOLLOWING afternoon. He rose from the seat in front of the pianoforte. "I love her."

"Who?" The dowager set down her embroidery and looked at her son in surprise. "I don't believe I've ever heard you utter those words."

"I never have. Before this, I didn't understand love. She made me return to my music, and I'm beginning to feel whole again. Only when she challenged me to play again was I ready to listen to such advice." He held out his hand toward the dowager. "Come, Mother, I know you'll be pleased to know that your conspiracies have worked. I'm going to marry Miss Rothwell, if she'll have me."

"Marion!" The dowager jumped up with an alacrity unusual at her age. "I couldn't be more pleased. But I thought she's marrying Sir Cedric."

"She told me herself that she has jilted Sir Cedric. She wouldn't tell me the reason, but at this point I don't care." He took the dowager's hand and pulled her toward the door. "You shall accompany me to Albemarle Street. While I speak with Sir Bertram, you shall calm Lady Winthrop. I don't want any scenes if they can be avoided."

With all due haste, the earl tooled the phaeton to the

Winthrop residence. The dowager pulled her cashmere shawl more tightly around her shoulders since an evening wind had brought a sudden chill.

The earl jumped down and assisted his parent. They knocked on the door.

"You should have made an appointment to see Sir Bertram ahead of time, Pierce."

A footman opened the door and let them inside. Fawley waited in the hallway. "Sir Bertram is not in at the moment, but I can deliver your card to Lady Winthrop."

Marion's aunt greeted them feebly as Fawley showed them to the blue salon. A layer of shawls swathed her from head to foot as she reclined on the chaise longue by the window. She invited them to sit down.

After the formal polite noises, the earl came right to the point. "I would like to see Miss Rothwell, if that's acceptable."

"But she's not here," said Lady Winthrop. "She left an hour ago with Sir Cedric and Melvin to view a horse that belongs to one of Sir Cedric's cronies."

They earl swore silently. "A disappointment. When will she be back home?"

"Oh, in time for supper, I suppose." Lady Winthrop waved her arm toward the tea tray. "You are staying for tea, I hope?"

The dowager rose. "I'm afraid there's no time for that. We have a dinner engagement later. Please tell Marion that we were here."

They said good-bye, and in the hallway a young countrified maid approached them cautiously. She was twisting her apron in an agitated manner, and the earl felt a premonition tickle the hairs on his neck. "Yes? Is there something we can do for you?"

"I'm Pansy, Miss Marion's . . . p-personal maid. I'm

afraid something dreadful might have happened to Miss Marion.''

''Dreadful?'' The earl suppressed an urge to shake the young girl.

The dowager stepped forward and spoke gently to Pansy. ''What happened? We're friends of Miss Marion. Tell us everything.''

Pansy wrung her hands. ''Sir Cedric came and threatened her. He said sumthin' awful would happen to her papa if she didn't come with him. That foppish cousin of hers said he'd help *if he got well paid.* Sir Cedric promised he would.''

''Where did they go?''

''I wus hidin' behind th' bedroom door when that Cousin Melvin forced her to leave. Sir Cedric said that sum cleric in a small town north would marry 'em quick as a cat swishes his tail.''

''Didn't she call out for help?'' the earl demanded to know.

''She was afeared that Sir Cedric would make good on his threat—and he would.'' Pansy chewed on her knuckles, then gave the dowager an entreating glance.

''They went north, and I didn't dare to tell Sir Bertram. He would have been ever so mad.''

''You're afraid of the Winthrops, aren't you, Pansy,'' the dowager said gently.

''They . . . they aren't very n-nice,'' Pansy said. ''They aren't kind to Miss Marion, not kind at all!''

The dowager placed a hand on the girl's shoulder. ''Try to remember the place where they were going.''

Pansy wrinkled her brow. ''Perhaps it was an estate, not a town, something like Dark . . . Dark . . . Da—''

''Dark Forest! Longpole's dilapidated estate,'' the earl said. ''Let's go, Mother.''

They set out as the sun was a dying orange glow on the

horizon. Pansy came rushing out with two blankets before the team left, then waved as the coach trundled down the street. The earl's chest clenched with worry. He had to be in time to save Marion . . .

Marion stared with dry, aching eyes at the setting sun. Not knowing what was going to happen next made her numb with apprehension. All the courage she had felt after winning back Laurel Manor on the previous evening had evaporated. A shudder of unease swept through her as she viewed her "jailers," Sir Cedric and the odious Melvin. She remembered the moment when they had forced her away from Albemarle Street and safety.

"Marion, I hope you'll be cooperative, or else your father will have an accident," Sir Cedric had threatened. "You come quietly on this trip, and at the end awaits every comfort you could ever desire."

Marion had glared at him and thought it was a tasteless joke. But no, he was serious. She knew he would carry out his threat. By now her fear had escalated, and her knees began to shake uncontrollably.

"We'll soon be there," Melvin said. His face shone with sudden perspiration, and Marion noticed that he was nervous.

A gleam of triumph shone in Sir Cedric's eyes. "Yes, we'll soon be rich, Melvin. Once I have Laurel Manor, you will be amply rewarded."

Marion had walked into the terrifying nightmare, hoping that someone would stop them, but here they were, going north.

She sat stiffly in the far corner so as not to suffer the touch of Sir Cedric's hands on her body. She kept avoiding his gaze, thus evading his smirk. If someone didn't come to her aid, she would be at the mercy of Sir Cedric's cruelty.

She wondered if Pansy had told anyone of this latest development . . .

"I have a terrible headache," she complained. The urgency to stall the rapid progress of the coach jabbed her constantly. "And I'm dying of thirst. If you don't let me eat soon, I'll have a fainting spell."

"Are you threatening us?" Melvin asked, his voice harsh with tension.

"Not at all, I only want some food." Marion shivered under his stare, and she clenched her teeth together to prevent them from clattering. To remember she had shared a roof with this "worm" for two and a half months made her skin prickle with revulsion.

The two men murmured between themselves, and Marion willed them to stop the coach.

"Very well, we can all do with a bit of sustenance. This trip was a trifle rushed, and we had no time to prepare," Sir Cedric said airily, as if the outing was a pleasure trip to Richmond.

Through the window, Sir Cedric ordered the coachman to stop at the next inn, which was located at Hatfield. Marion leaned her head against the squabs and moaned softly, eyeing her tormentors from under her eyelashes.

"What's amiss, Marion? I have never seen you display such weakness before," Melvin commented in a disgusted voice.

"This time you've gone too far, Mel, but I'll not retaliate by putting toads in your bed. I've grown out of such pranks. Not that you have, but I hope I won't have to suffer your presence much longer. I've changed; I've grown up, but you haven't."

Melvin sucked in his breath. "Dashed nonsense. You shall pay for this."

Marion wanted to stall for time so that someone could

have a chance to find her. Or she might find a way to escape. A moment's despair flashed through her as she wondered again if Pansy had told anyone about her predicament.

The coach halted with a jolt in front of the inn, and Marion was thrown to the opposite seat right onto Sir Cedric's lap. Flailing her arms, she struggled to disengage herself from his offensive embrace, but Sir Cedric only held her against his chest.

"Let go of me, you—you toad!" Marion jabbed an elbow hard in his middle, and he groaned with the sudden pain.

"Marion is a handful of problems, Cedric. Are you sure you want to go through with the wedding?" Melvin sounded doubtful as he witnessed Marion's flare of temper.

Sir Cedric laughed. "I have struggled and humiliated myself this long to receive Marion's hand in marriage; I damned well will go through with it! She needs a lesson, and I'm just the one to give it to her." He glared at her. "Jaunting about town with lofty airs in the company of earls and countesses doesn't suit you, Marion. You will see that country life, taking care of my mansion, rearing my children, will suit you to perfection."

Sir Cedric turned his annoyed expression on Melvin. "Your father has been much too lenient with her, letting her go about town with only her maid in tow. That will have to be changed." He pinched her waist, and Marion punched him hard across the nose with her fist. To her contentment she noticed that she'd drawn blood. His nails dug into her like talons, but he let go of his hold abruptly as blood started trickling down his face. She huddled in the corner, as far away from him as possible. What would he do now?

Holding a handkerchief against his nose, he muttered, "Devil take you, Marion! I believe we should not postpone the wedding, but execute it at this very inn. We will surely find some willing country parson to perform the duty. I cannot wait to punish you for this.'' He waved the special license that he'd procured earlier in the morning from his uncle, the Archbishop.

Marion froze. He couldn't mean it!

He did. She saw it in the fulminating glance he threw her as he stepped down from the coach. ''You stay here until everything is settled. I will have food delivered here on a tray.'' To Melvin he said, ''You keep a steady eye on her or you'll be sorry.''

Sir Cedric stalked off toward the taproom, and Marion stole a glance at her cousin. His skin had a yellowish tint and was shiny with perspiration.

''How can you let him do this, Mel? You should be ashamed of yourself. My father would kill you if he knew what you have done to me.'' Two hot tears trickled down her cheeks.

He looked guilty, fidgeted on his seat, and cast repeated glances toward the inn. ''I simply had to. My gambling debts are mounting, and I have to pay them before someone calls me out. Now shut your mouth, Marion,'' he ordered brusquely.

She took a deep breath to speak her mind, but his fist knotted in the air, threatening her. She silenced. It was no use reasoning with Melvin. He'd never liked her, and he would never care what happened to her.

A fat maid ambled across the dusty yard with a heavy tray. Reaching the door she spoke through the window. ''I 'ear Her Ladyship's sick, so I brought ye a good soup of peas and pork and some black bread. I 'ope 'twill restore yer spirits.''

Marion's stomach turned at the thought of pork and peas simmering in lard, but she put a good face on and smiled bleakly. Should she beg the maid for help?

The maid spoke to Melvin. "We 'eard she's outta 'er mind because 'er weddin' was postponed. Th' good gentleman inside is goin' to see our parson for assistance. 'Ow very romantic ter 'ave a weddin' at th' inn!" She clapped her fat palms together, and Marion wanted to pour the contents of the soup bowl over her head and offer her the place beside Sir Cedric in front of the parson. This innocent maid could not see the wolf in sheep's clothing that hovered in her taproom.

With dying airs Marion spoke. "I would need a room to refresh myself. Could you convey my wishes to the wol–gentleman in the shee—taproom, please." She proceeded to flutter her hands in front of her face in a helpless fashion.

"O' course, milady, she needs a few minutes to tidy 'er 'air, I suppose." The maid sent a critical glance at Marion's mussed curls and spectacles. Curtsying, she took herself off in a hurry, only to return one minute later, flustered.

"Milady is to follow me. I wus ordered, if you please, to keep yer' company th' whole while."

Relieved, Marion stepped out of the suffocating carriage. The maid stared dubiously at Marion's gray morning dress, one of Aunt Adele's relics.

"Not wut I'd call a weddin' gown, if ye don't mind me sayin' so." She resolutely led Marion into the inn.

A peabrain, Marion thought. All through the hour Marion spent refreshing herself she tried to get rid of the maid, without avail. The poor girl didn't know of Marion's burning desire to escape, but prattled on endlessly. Marion sipped the potent ale, served to her in a tankard, to slake the terrible thirst parching her throat.

A hard knock sounded on the door, and Melvin stuck his head around the corner. "I'm here to escort you downstairs to the private parlor. The local vicar was persuaded to perform the ceremony and is at this very moment on his way here."

Marion's thoughts darted to possible escape routes, but as if Melvin read her thoughts, he availed himself of her arm and pulled her brusquely out of the chamber.

The private parlor was stifling hot, and Marion gasped in aversion at the sight of Sir Cedric, who received her with a leer. Her throat constricted and the cramped room seemed to shrink around her. A cold sweat broke out all over her body, and she gripped the edge of the door to steady her reeling senses. Her legs turned into a jellylike substance, and she breathed deeply to regain control. *Is this going to be the awful end of a disastrous day?*

While Marion was struggling to recover her composure, the rotund vicar entered the premises. With a false smile plastered to his lips, Sir Cedric stepped forward to greet the newcomer. He proceeded to introduce them all. Then he pushed a few coins into the cleric's pudgy hand.

Marion swallowed convulsively to wet her dry throat, and she gazed in despair at the jolly person in front of her.

"Ah, the blushing maid is afeared—and one should be when taking such an important step in life." He lifted her chin with one sweaty finger. "A fiery little thing." Turning back to Sir Cedric, he asked, "And do you have a special license?"

Sir Cedric eagerly handed him a neatly folded paper.

"Ah, we can commence the ceremony. Alas, there will be no flowers to delight the eyes, no family and friends to witness the act, but when the knot is tied, it is a sacred thing—something we only do once in a lifetime. Shall we call in a couple of witnesses?"

Marion froze to the spot as she watched the plump prattle box and a thin hostler enter the room. If she didn't do something soon, she would be married to Sir Cedric, the

Clodpole. Their faces began to undulate in front of her eyes. She took two faltering steps and fell headlong into the baffled vicar's arms. He tripped and toppled backward under her weight. Marion stared wild-eyed at him, not quite understanding what was happening to her. For the first time in her life she was fainting! The realization jolted her out of the spell, and she struggled to her feet. She was too weak to fight as Sir Cedric pinned her to his side.

"Let's go on with the ceremony!"

Among the notable whips of London, the earl's matched grays were known to have exceptional stamina. They did their best now to bear the earl and his mother out of London at breakneck speed. But even first-class horseflesh needs to rest, and the earl had to stop at a posting inn and change horses, getting cattle that was a far cry from the grays in speed. Gritting his teeth, the earl sped on, not even allowing himself a glass of ale.

The traffic thinned the farther they left London behind, and he stopped at every inn to inquire if a private traveling chaise had pulled in. He reaped nothing but negative answers, except at one posting house, where Longpole had changed horses.

When the fresh set of nags began to show signs of fatigue, Litton was fearing the worst. They had obviously hastened directly to Dark Forest, Longpole's country seat in Hertford.

When he felt as hot and thirsty as the horses, he had to stop at the next inn. Lo and behold! In the middle of the yard stood the Longpole carriage.

Anger fueling him, the earl flung the ribbons to a boy in the stable yard and raced into the taproom. Leaning over the counter, he gripped the landlord by the lapels of his corduroy vest. "Is there a young lady here with red hair and spectacles? Answer me, you clod!'' The earl had no time for niceties when every second was of the essence.

''Ye must mean th' bride. They are gettin' on with the ceremony right now in th' private parlor. I wouldn't disturb 'em if I were you,'' the landlord muttered, resenting the earl's harsh treatment.

The earl did not stop to discuss the pros and cons of entering the private parlor. He practically tore the door off its hinges and hurled himself inside. The dowager followed at a more leisurely pace.

CHAPTER 18

TWO PEOPLE WERE SPRAWLED ON THE FLOOR, MARION AND A MAN who appeared to be a country parson. Sir Cedric took two steps toward the earl, his eyes narrowed to wrathful slits and his hands balled into fists. Pierce's gaze alighted on Marion, who lay crumpled in a heap, and without paying the slightest heed to Sir Cedric, he neatly sidestepped the oncoming punch and knelt beside her.

She moaned softly as he lifted her head from the floor.

"Stand up and fight like a man!" Sir Cedric demanded, delivering a wicked blow from behind to the earl's ear.

The earl winced, the air temporarily forced out of him from the pain. Potent wrath grew to a suffocating wave in his chest and he stood, after gently lowering Marion back down. The dowager kneeled beside her as the earl challenged Sir Cedric.

Receiving another jab to his ear, the earl saw red. With a rough jerk he gripped Sir Cedric's collar and lifted him off his feet.

"You will have more bruises than you can count when I'm finished with you," he snarled and flung the younger man roughly out the door. "And we're going outside, since I want to spare the ladies from slipping on your blood."

Sir Cedric stumbled on the stone step and fell headlong

into the dust. Coughing and spitting, he rose, his face livid with rage. The earl had barely time to step down before Sir Cedric's body smashed severely into his. They both tumbled to the ground, but the earl was the first back on his feet. He delivered a blinding right hook to Sir Cedric's jaw.

"Blast it!" Sir Cedric staggered backward, and he shook his head in pain. Roaring, he advanced on Litton with both fists up, only to receive another stone-hard blow to his chin. He dropped to the ground with a grunt, hitting his nose on the hard-packed dirt. Blood spurted freely from that offended organ, and Sir Cedric remained lying, his strength spent.

Disgusted, the earl turned away, kicking up a cloud of dust that settled on Sir Cedric's head. He stalked into the inn after brushing off his clothes.

The thin hostler sat on top of Melvin's back, hindering that man's breathing as his face pressed into a dusty carpet. Melvin's neck shone purple, and his breath made a rattling sound in his throat.

"Get off your perch, fellow," the earl ordered the hostler. He bent down and raised Melvin by the scruff of his neck. Then he delivered a blow that fell Melvin back onto the floor in a faint. "Don't you ever dare to speak with Marion again," the earl said to the still form.

The earl tenderly lifted Marion, who opened sleepy eyes. "I'm so tired," she slurred. Her eyes flew open, "Pierce? Is that really you?" Her arms wound happily around his neck. "How I prayed that you would arrive in time! You did, didn't you?" Her head slumped against his chest and she sighed contentedly.

The earl ordered the gaping maid to show them to a private parlor and then make some strong coffee. She complied in awed silence, and Litton could place his precious burden down on the sofa. Folding a blanket over

Marion, he left the room to make sure the villains had learned their lesson.

The dowager found a vinaigrette in her reticule and pressed it to Marion's nose. "I'm glad we arrived in time to stop this ordeal."

Marion blinked. "I'm speechless with relief." She pressed the dowager's hand. "I'm grateful you're here to act as chaperone. From now on, I want to do what is proper. I want to be a real lady, not an untamed pony."

The dowager laughed. "Who called you that?"

"Aunt Adele."

"I assure you, there isn't much of that left, and I'm perhaps a little sad to see the pony go."

Marion laughed and hugged her friend, and perhaps future mother-in-law?

The earl viewed the two young men who sat on the wooden bench in the taproom, Sir Cedric still pressing a handkerchief against his nose.

"Well, boys, I hope you've leaned your lesson," the earl said, bracing his boot against the bench. "If you ever touch Miss Marion again, you'll have to answer to me. Is that understood?"

The two young men nodded sullenly. The earl brushed the dust off his trousers and returned to the private parlor.

Marion sat propped against a pillow sipping the coffee that the maid had delivered. There was no sign of the dowager, and Marion suspected she had left them alone on purpose.

"Feeling better?" he asked.

"A little. I only want to sleep." She proceeded to yawn widely.

"Did you have something to drink here?" he asked. At Marion's affirmative nod, he said, "Sir Cedric must have laced your drink with a sleeping draught—to make you more cooperative."

Marion smiled warmly. "Thank you for rescuing me. It just occurred to me that I had my revenge, after all, my revenge on both you and Sir Cedric. I beat you both at piquet."

"Only once, but never again," the earl said with a laugh.

Her vision blurred and she struggled to stay awake. Pushing her feet over the side of the sofa, she rose on shaky legs. The earl was at her side instantly. His strong arm went around her waist, and she had to look into his eyes. An arrested look had invaded their depths. Marion wanted to drown from the bliss of being in his embrace. She noted his lips closing the distance to hers, and she waited in breathless expectation for him. His mouth was hot and demanding on hers. A warm spiraling sensation filled her, and she could hardly know what was dream and what was reality. She clung to him, wanting the kiss to go on forever.

He lifted his head at last, and her world slowly righted itself. He watched her, his eyes brimming with tenderness. "I was so worried that I had lost you." He took a deep breath. "I slept well last night—for the first time in weeks. I feel as if a weighty worry in my chest has dissolved, and I've never felt lighter. All thanks to you."

"Someone had to give you permission to start your music again."

"No . . . it's much more than that." He eagerly cupped her chin with one hand. "In you, I've found my destiny. You must know I can't wait to call you mine, stripling. I love you. I believe I loved you from the first, although I had no idea. I've been such a blind fool."

His lips roved hungrily across hers and whispered against her mouth. "Tell me you accept my offer, dearest Marion," he urged.

"I do. I have always loved you, Pierce, but I will soon bore you to death."

"No risk of that. Between you and Prinny, I will have my hands full." His tongue found her ear, and Marion squirmed with pleasure.

"You don't mind my hair and spectacles, and you don't think that I'm ten years old—and what about this latest scandal?"

"The tattlemongers need a new juicy scandal to tear apart."

Marion furrowed her brow. "What will Uncle Bertram say when he finds out . . . ?"

"I'll deal with him; don't you worry." He kissed a burnished curl. "Ahhh, you're adorable, every inch of you, and my blood is boiling with madness; in fact, I want to make love to you right now."

"Oh, Pierce—I love you—stop . . . you're . . . tickling . . . my ear."

His second kiss was even more dizzying than the first, and Marion wondered where it could have led if the door hadn't opened behind them.

"Aha!" cried the dowager with a smile. "Caught you red-handed."

The earl released Marion reluctantly. He'd never known such soaring happiness. "She's agreed to become my wife, Mother."

"I knew she would." The dowager winked. "You'll be very happy together. Pierce, I knew you would fall in love when the right lady came into your life."

The earl gave a foolish grin. "Marion's more than a lady; she's a blessing."

"Well, we'd better head back to London and plan a grand wedding. If I have my way, it'll be the most spectacular of the Season," said the dowager.

"Mother, you always have your way."

Blissful, Marion sat between Dot and her beloved in the phaeton. With her head cradled against his shoulder, the earl tooled the equipage toward London—and the future, a future that showed a lot of promise.